William E. Easton

Dessalines

A dramatic tale. A single chapter from Haiti's history

William E. Easton

Dessalines
A dramatic tale. A single chapter from Haiti's history

ISBN/EAN: 9783337393601

Printed in Europe, USA, Canada, Australia, Japan

Cover: Foto ©Andreas Hilbeck / pixelio.de

More available books at **www.hansebooks.com**

DESSALINES

A DRAMATIC TALE

––––––

A SINGLE CHAPTER FROM HAITI'S

HISTORY

BY

WILLIAM EDGAR EASTON

––––––

J. W. Burson-Company, Publishers

1893

THIS VOLUME IS LOVINGLY DEDICATED
TO MY ELDEST DAUGHTER,

ATHENAIS MARIE EASTON,

THAT SHE MAY BE ENCOURAGED SOME DAY TO
JOIN THE LITERATI OF THE RACE AND
WIELD A POTENT PEN IN BEHALF
OF THE NEW EMANCIPATION.

THE AUTHOR.

PREFACE

It is with much diffidence I submit to the crucial test of public criticism a work which is apt to be provocative of the harshest strictures, but I will feel fully repaid should Dessalines have accomplished the author's purpose of attracting the attention of the literati of the race to the rich fields of dramatic and narrative art, which by every right are distinctly the property of the Negro.

A nation or race have other legal possessions aside from those whose geographic limitations are its boundaries of rivers, lakes and mountains. Dearer than all else should be its tradition, history, literature and music, for upon the proper education of the masses in these requisites depends durability of that race or nation's fame and its guarantee of future greatness. It is only on these solid bedrocks we can hope to build up a healthy and substantial race pride.

The Mongolian has his art, music and literature ; the Semitic race likewise. The Caucasian boy at his mother's feet learns, with pride, of the deeds of his race and, through the spirit of emulation, raises the standard of the living above the ashes of the dead. The Negro alone fails to immortalize his distinguished

dead, and leaves to the prejudiced pen of other
races, the office, which, by a proper conception of
duty to posterity, very properly becomes his duty.
What religious pen of the race has written of Bene-
dict, the Moor; of the sainted Africans, Monica and
Augustine; or sang in stately verse the deeds of the
heroic Haitiens; or sought to turn the light of truth
on the historic greatness of ancient Ethiope?

How many of our children and their children will
know that the Dumas were of their race and Russia's
greatest poet had the blood of the down-trodden in
his veins? It is true we have had our biographers and
able writers on politico-economics; but we have sig-
nally failed to produce one genius gifted writer of
Negro fiction; one writer of Negro drama; one poet
whose lyre plays the sweetest airs in the land of his
Afric sires.

Especially with us has the art of drama writing
been neglected. This fact is more deplorable when
we pause to consider the potent influence the drama
wields in the reformation or vitiation of public
opinion. In ancient Rome the drama was made the
reformer of private vices and public morals. On the
mimic stage were portrayed the direful results of the
abuse of power, and kings were made acquainted with
the needs of their subjects. The stage in those days,
as it is today, was a mirror for despots to view their
own iniquity.

It is true we have our sketch artists, whose business it has been to supply our burnt-cork "artists"

with ideas. Indeed, we have had excellent carica-
turists of the Negro, in his only recognized school of
legitimate drama, *i. e.*, buffoonery.

But the author of this work hopes to see a happier
era inaugurated by the constant production of legitimate drama, written exclusively for Negro players
and meeting, he hopes, with the full endorsement of
the brother in white.

Othello, once the pride of the ambitious colored
histrionic, has sadly metamorphosed his once singu-
larly dark complexion and now holds the boards, the
victim of a very mild case of sunburn.

How we have degenerated ! Poor old Uncle Tom
may yet play the banjo and "pat time" for the now
thoroughly civilized Topsey, who, when last heard
from, was "spouting poetry" and "giving" the skirt
dance.

The Negro jubilee singer meets the brother-in-
white's approval ; but a black Romeo, a black Mel-
notte ! Ye gods, protect the black Proteans from the
weight of popular white disapproval. Voice and
gesture, they declare, are not all the proprieties.

For the reasons, as above enumerated, has the
author presumed to lay on the altar of race pride the
dramatic tale of the heroic Dessalines. Let the
critic with a charitable hand separate its history from
romance and give the author the credit, at least, of
seeking, in the way he knows best, to teach the truth,
that " minds are not made captive by slavery's chains,
nor were men's souls made for barter and trade."

To the many talented histrionics of the race :
Dessalines is only a " pointer " to the literati. To
my brothers of the press : Treat your erring brother
kindly.   Yours, for the race,

WILLIAM E. EASTON.

Galveston, Tex., Jan. 20, 1893.

DRAMATIS PERSONÆ.

BLACKS.	COLORED.
DESSALINES.	RIGAUD.
DOMINIQUE.	LEFEBRE.
PETOU.	FLAVIEN.
ANDRÉ.	CLARISSE.
PIERRE.	SOLDIERS.
PLACIDE.	
MÈRE MARGERET.	
SLAVES AND SOLDIERS.	

ACT I

DESSALINES.

ACT I

SCENE 1.

[PLANTATION OF DU MARTIN.   TIME—5 A. M.)

Enter FLAVIEN.

FLAVIEN.

Five o'clock, and the lazy slaves are still abed.   It
is only of late they have become such sluggards.   Indeed, there must be some infernal conspiracy afloat,
as the masters, all over the island, are complaining
something is amiss.   Now, what that something is,
cudgels my brain.   [*Enter* PLACIDE.]   So, knave,
thou art out of bed !

PLACIDE.

Bed ?

FLAVIEN.

Yes, bed. What wouldst thou have me call it?

PLACIDE.

Out of the graves of the masters, out of the devil, if it please thee.

FLAVIEN.

Thou art impertinent, knave Placide; a hundred lashes will be thy portion, should I have cause to teach thee milder manners.

PLACIDE.

And I, good Flavien, had I the chance—Mon Dieu!—I would give thee and every accursed mulatre—

FLAVIEN.

What?

PLACIDE.

Death.

FLAVIEN.

Forget not, slave, I am thy master's—

PLACIDE.

Pimp.

FLAVIEN.

[*Striking him down with handle of whip.*] Take that, infernal black !

PLACIDE.

[*Arising.*] Every blustering coward sees the rise and setting of his sun. [*Exit.*

Enter Slaves singing "Vive La Liberte." Seeing FLAVIEN *they cease singing, with the exception of* PETOU.

PETOU.

Citizens, keep it up ! Vive la—[*Sees* FLAVIEN]— la mort et mille tounerres !

FLAVIEN.

Ump ! What means this ?

PETOU.

I will tell thee. We have just heard the news. Toussaint is on the road with ten thousand blacks to set us free ! We are going to be citizens !

FLAVIEN.

Indeed ! Ye will be angels some day, if ye are only true and faithful servants. Above all things, guard against such a spirit as is in the black hulk of your fellow-servant, Placide. This very day did he dare call me—the natural son and overseer of your master— a pimp.

SLAVES.

Ha ! ha !

FLAVIEN.

Ye dare laugh at such an insult to me ?

PIERRE.

Good Flavien, is it not true, that on the night of fête des fleurs thou forced the daughter of Mère Antoinette to a liaison with the master ?

FLAVIEN.

Is she not the property of her master, to do with as he wills?   Knaves, what higher ambition should the slave possess than to infect the master's blood with the degradation of his own?   What prouder title can your mothers bear, than mother to your mas ter's child.

PETOU.

I wish every master's child were in purgatory.

FLAVIEN.

To thy fields !   Why should I deign to parley with your kind.   Only this, at sunset, from my own hand,

shall Placide receive an hundred lashes. [*Exit*
SLAVES.] It is hard enough to bear the slights of
the master and his kin, without having to endure the
contempt of his slaves. Three years in Paris have
made me a discontented man, and the remainder of
my life in Haiti will be a foretaste of hell. Un
mulatre, drawn from the carcass of a slave, by the
unrighteous process of the master, is a human given
to the world unable to bear the ostracism of racial
prejudice and capable of every slavish hatred. But
this thing cannot, must not, last, for with the intrepid
Rigaud our confrêres will gain franchisement. What
can we waste upon our sires? I hate them no less
than I despise—and in an unnatural manner, too—
the mother that gave me birth.

[*Enter* DESSALINES.]

DESSALINES.

Such sentiment become thy kind.

FLAVIEN.

What, Dessalines! Thou here?

DESSALINES.

Ay, dog; I am here—Monsieur Dessalines, the
freedman; made so by his own hand and proclama-
tion. Or, if it suit thy quaking spirit better—I am
thy master's escaped slave. Take me, if thou darest!

FLAVIEN.

Why didst thou return, knave? Where is thy hiding place?

DESSALINES.

Hiding place! My castle is on the mountains, where dwells no will save mine, and no slave dare breathe the air and refuse to be a free man.

FLAVIEN.

Thou art then a Maroon?

DESSALINES.

Ay, one of those self-freed, much-feared fugitives, who love liberty and hate the masters. Who, not satisfied with merely breathing words of hatred, wreak vengeance on them for their wrongs upon the race. Of my bold lances there is not one who has not purged his soul of slavish servitude in the blood of some accursed white! Fear not thy kind last; we are not jackal.

FLAVIEN.

Good Dessalines, thou art in no good humor today.

DESSALINES.

Good Dessalines—good slave! I remember when first I was sent to the master to receive from his

lips my first instructions in the art of making self, in
all things, subservient to the master's will. On en-
trance to his presence, in meek and humble tones, I
showed my aptitude for the first lesson in slavish
servitude. This must have pleased the good man,
for next he tried to instill in me that God expected
of the slave obedience to the master's will. From
sundry books he had at hand he read to me; and
all he read impressed me with the thought that the
gods from the beginning had ordained one race to
serve, the other race to rule. My people were of
that race to serve; his people of the race to rule.
Desiring to see how far this mockery went, I asked
to be taught a prayer whereby I could free my soul
from guilt of insolence and hatred to the whites. He
directed me to say a prayer, which, after him I re-
peated, and called on all the saints and angels of his
faith to witness I was an obdurate, worthless sinner.
Again did he seek to impress me with the thought,
I must learn to love the masters. Then threw I my
mask aside. I told him I hated the masters and
their gods! I told him the African's gods taught revenge for wrongs, hatred for hatred and death for
death! On this he threatened me with chastisement,
torment and the church's most fruitful curses. He
dared to call me a pagan dog! Dost know what
then I did? I plucked him by his unholy beard,
threw him to the ground and spurned him as I
would some snarling, fangless cur.

FLAVIEN.

God have mercy on thee ! Sacreligious wretch !

DESSALINES.

Ha ! ha !

FLAVIEN.

Ignorant as thou art, thou must know the enormity of thy offense in the sight of God.

DESSALINES.

Thou, too, art a doler out of superstitious cant—an humble worshipper of thy master's household gods. I have none—I know none and owe allegiance only to my kind. A race enslaved, 'tis true, but not all of us are only fit to be in spirit as thy master hath made thee. Teach the slave if he disobey he receives the lash. 'Tis in reason, for thy corporal frame is captive ; but to command the mind to worship at an altar where the sacrifice of liberty and manhood occur each day, is as tyrannical as useless. Minds are not made captive with slavery chains, nor are men's souls made for barter and trade.

FLAVIEN.

There is no reason in thy talk !

DESSALINES.

Reason does not suit thy kind; if 'twere otherwise what justification could we find to slay thee.

FLAVIEN.

It is safe to bay an unarmed man.

DESSALINES.

[*Casting a dagger at Flavien's feet.*] I'll share my arms with thee and name thee : The platter-licker of thy master's household. Thou claimst race with those who rule, and I, a full blood African, dare thee to mortal combat !

FLAVIEN.

I have no quarrel with thee.

DESSALINES.

Ay, not with me ; but with thy father's nerveless slaves. Thy courage is the coward's courage, born of a knowledge of the weakness of thy adversary.

FLAVIEN.

Braggart and insulter, leave this plantation ere I summon help to make thee leave !

DESSALINES.

Thy commands would be as idle jests wert thou to utter them. I go ; but 'tis my pleasure.

FLAVIEN.

It is thy pleasure to be boastful of thy prowess.

DESSALINES.

It is my pleasure [*Chokes* FLAVIEN] to throttle thee as I would some necessary fowl !

FLAVIEN.

Help ! Help ! [*Enter* SLAVES, *stand undeter-mined.*] [DESSALINES *casts* FLAVIEN *aside.*] Take yonder ruffian ! Why stand ye there like idiots ?

DESSALINES.

He has called thee slaves. Look upon him whining like some currish hound—his master's spawn without a necessary resemblance to that master or claim upon the suffrage of yourselves. Look upon him ! He half and half, and I full black, and tell me who is master here !

SLAVES.

Thou art !

DESSALINES.

What has made me master here? What will
make ye masters here? Is his white tainted flesh un-
vulnerable? Look upon us! I am as black as the
shadows of night, with muscles of iron and a will
that never was enslaved! What has he that I have
not, save the arrogance of the accursed Caucasian
blood? What hath these Franks that we are their
household chattel—that we are their beasts? They
suffer from the heat more than we, their sight is less
keen, the evening dews hasten them to their graves
and the noonday's sun finds them under cover. The
very fibres of their frames are weak and puny, and,
as the gods allotted labor for the part of man, they
must depend on us to carry out the law. What
fetich have they that sustains their power to rule and
ours to serve? We are ten to one their number now
in Haiti—perhaps an hundred, it may be. Then is it
the strong who rules, or is it the natural sequence of
our own inward weakness? Have ye mothers, sisters
or laughing babes ye can call your own?

SLAVES.

We are only slaves.

DESSALINES.

Were ye always thus and your sires, too? Or
must it follow ye must always be?

SLAVES.

So it doth appear.

DESSALINES.

Listen ! When but a stripling, in my native land, I was wont to hunt the great king of the jungles, whose roar is like the distant thunder and whose bite is death. One day, with five companions, armed with spears and shields, I penetrated a dense undergrowth and suddenly confronted a lioness and her male. On seeing us they gave forth terrific roars in defiance of our arms and numbers. All unprepared for the meeting, my companions were affrighted and would have fled had I not called on them to halt— as flight meant a fearful death—and charge upon the foe. We charged upon them, and, though they were wounded, they were not disabled and only made more fierce and desperate. Then ensued there such a battle ! The spears were torn from our hands ! Three of my companions with their entrails protruding from their torn abdomens were still in death upon the ground ! The brutes' terrific roar and fearful carnage drove terror to our hearts, and, routed, we ran ingloriously from the scene. What would I teach thee from this tale ? The same lesson I have learnt : That wavering is cowardice and desperation makes men brave ; that the arms of the oppressors, however great in number, cannot prevail with the desperation of the lion at bay. The masters are wavering like the tall palmetto in the storm's angry blast. Let us but be brave and the shackles now upon your limbs will be turned to anklets of gold and precious stones, taken from the bodies of these Frankish dogs. If ye would be brutes, be lions !

SLAVES.

Wise Dessalines !

DESSALINES.

Ye do me honor, messieurs.

PETOU.

Dieu et mon droit ! He calls us sirs !

DESSALINES.

Free men, then ! If so, follow me !

SLAVES.

Ay, we would be free !

PETOU.

That rhymes with liberté—let me see—whiskey.

FLAVIEN.

Curses on thee ! Thou wilt rue me this day.

DESSALINES.

My blessings abide with thee, good Flavien. Au revoir.   [*Curtain.*

SCENE 2.

[STUDY IN LEFEBRE'S HOME, AT PORT AU PRINCE. TIME— EVENING. LEFEBRE READING PAPER.]

LEFEBRE.

It is tedious to be forced to await the news of our fate from the assembly of our enemies. There is nothing in the Courier des Mondes to give us the least grain of hope that the statesmen, press and people of France will disagree with the colonials and recognize us other than as emancipated slaves, destitute of every right of suffrage, who should thank heaven they are allowed to exist even as such.

[*Enter* RIGAUD.]

RIGAUD.

Bon jour, mon comrade! As ever I see searching the columns of the Courier for news of our speedy enfranchisement.

LEFEBRE.

News, I sometimes fear, will never reach Haiti.

RIGAUD.

But eventually it must come, even if we are forced to demand our rights through the dense cloud of cannon smoke and at the point of the sword.

LEFEBRE.

Hush ! We know not who may hear.

RIGAUD.

And who hears, hears not too soon. If it be impossible with such a champion as Lafayette to gain favorable recognition of our rights from the assemblies, from what other source save a contest of arms can we hope to prove victorious. Nay, interrupt me not. Have not mes confrêres and I crossed the ocean twice to plead before the haughty French for the establishment of our claims? What has been their invariable reply? Hath it not been : "Return to Haiti, we will consider your appeals." Ay, they did consider them most favorably, the colonials protested and France's weak pretense to do us justice died a nurseling. Thou art not satisfied with this child's coaxing ; neither I nor forty thousand other natural heirs to every right a Frenchman enjoys upon this island.

LEFEBRE.

My dear friend, do not think because by tempera-
ment I am less warm than thee; I am less willing to
venture everything in the struggle that lies before us.

RIGAUD.

Nay, I believe thou art as true as true can be, but
words of caution madden me. It is liberty, civil and
political, we want, and not caution! The time for
Parisian phrases and honied terms is passed. I have
considered this question in all its phases. The
French will awake to a true sense of duty only when
moved by steel and shot. [*Seats himself.*]

LEFEBRE.

Ah! I had forgotten; here is a letter for thee.

RIGAUD.

A strange undecipherable hand. [*Tears envelope.*]
Ah! It is from Monplaisir—per jailor, Cape Fran-
çois. [*Reads letter.*] Mon Dieu! The French have
spilt the first blood; they have opened a fountain
head that will flood and crimson the fertile soil of
Haiti! Pauvre Martinet! pauvre nous! Thou shalt
not go unavenged.

LEFEBRE.

What, the noble Martinet dead?

RIGAUD.

Dead. But the cause of human rights still marches on.

LEFEBRE.

Indeed, indeed, our cause looks hopeless.

RIGAUD.

Never! The spirit of Ogé and Martinet will fan he flame of freedom never yet quenched by tyranny and assassination.

[*Blast of trumpet without. Enter French Soldier.*]

SOLDIER.

General Leclerc sends greetings to Messieurs Rigaud, Lefebre and confrêres : prays heavens most bountiful gifts may be showered on them, bespeaking their loyalty to their father's government, sends herewith this commission.

RIGAUD.

Great cause have we for loyalty to France.

LEFEBRE.

Thou, sir, can retire within easy call. [*Exit* SOLDIER.]

RIGAUD.

What have we here?   More French hypocrisy !

LEFEBRE.

A perusal of this will show.   [*Breaks seal and reads.*]   "To Messrs. Rigaud, Lefebre and Confrères, Greeting: Know ye by these presents that the slaves throughout Haiti have arisen in arms against their masters and with torch and sword they are devastating this fair island.   Thousands of these blacks are now in arms lead by such blood-thirsty leaders as Dessalines and Christophe.   They threaten to burn Port au Prince and put to the sword its citizens. Moreover, they contemplate repelling the landing of French troops, who are now on shipboard in your bay.   France calls on you to assist in subjugating the rebellious blacks, and as some slight recompense for your effort, grants you every recognition for which you are petitioners before the French assembly. In proof of her good will and sincerity Monsieur Rigaud is herewith commissioned chief recruiting officer and general of infantry in the militaty service of France.   A higher honor at one bound no white Frenchman could aspire to.   Yours, etc.,

General Leclerc,
Acting Commander, Count de Rochembeau.

RIGAUD.

So soon hath my phophesy come true !

LEFEBRE.

We will, of course, to the support of France?

RIGAUD.

Rather will we be avenged on France for her neg-
lect and inhumanity.

LEFEBRE.

Certainly, thou wouldst not think it well to join the
blacks?

RIGAUD.

And why not? What confidence can we place in
a government which, with all its fair promises, stoops
to murder the messenger of its petitioners?

LEFEBRE.

But what can we hope to gain by affiliation with
the blacks? We have nothing in common. They
are envious of us—literally hate us; while we—we
despise them.

RIGAUD.

Their hatred is of our own making.

LEFEBRE.

Nevertheless, its intensity is so great, should they
succeed, and that, too, with our assistance, drunk

with victory, we would next fall victims to their un-
restrained passions! Our present state, deplorable
as it is, would be a thousand times more preferable
to the one we would find ourselves in, should the
slaves succeed in their fools' warfare. Where the interests are at variance and confidence is lacking, there
can be no combined effort that will lead to a desirable result.

RIGAUD.

Thy prejudices enlarge upon thy fears. A common cause would make us friends indeed !

LEFEBRE.

An undying, unquenchable hatred exists, as thou
knowest, between the blacks and men of color, whose
ardor centuries can not cool. Oh, Rigaud, let not thy
anger stand 'twixt thee and reason ! Go—be a lamb,
if thou wilt. Lie down with the wolf, but thou wilt
never rise with the sun at morn to bid thy ferocious
bedfellow a bon matin. As for me, God forbid, I
should love our French oppressors, but I would a
thousand times rather see this fair island as it is than
to live to view the blacks' domination.

RIGAUD.

Lefebre, thou reasonst well. Forgive me if I for
a moment faltered in assuming my proper place in
this contest of principles. This time shall we confide

in France, and if in our hour of need she fail us, on ourselves let the blame rest heaviest.

LEFEBRE.

Spoken like a patriot ! Repugnant as is the task before us, let us do it like men, who, in desperate straits, find strategy the only course open to them. Dictate—I will write.

[*Seats himself at table, pen in hand.*

RIGAUD.

Allons ! "General Leclerc, I accept thy commission and pledge the support of my confréres to the government of France. All we ask in return is that France be as loyal to her word as we are to ours. I await further orders. Rigaud." There !

LEFEBRE.

Enough. I will summon the guard.

LEFEBRE *opens door.* PETOU *brushes in by him and makes* RIGAUD *an elaborate salute.*

RIGAUD.

What wouldst thou here? My time belongs to France.

PETOU.

Thy time will soon be up then.

RIGAUD.

Camest thou here, knave, for idle jests?

PETOU.

God forbid! Thou art General Rigaud?

RIGAUD.

I am he.

PETOU.

I am a military man too.

RIGAUD.

Indeed!

PETOU.

Of course; everybody is military now.

RIGAUD.

Cease thy uncalled for remarks! Tell me thy business at once.

PETOU.

First must I introduce myself. I have the great satisfaction, sir—without pay—to be socius to Monsgr. Alphonse de Trop Dominique, the High Lord Chancellor—that expects to be—to his puissant highness,

Dessalines, generalissimo of the black troups of Haiti. Ahem !

RIGAUD.

What bombast !   Thy business, sirrah !

PETOU.

I have a message for thee.   Thou hath a sister— one Clarisse.

RIGAUD.

Aye ; what of her ?

PETOU.

Well, she is not at home.

RIGAUD.

[*Grabs him by the throat.*]   Dog of a slave, make thy meaning clear, or thy life shall pay the forfeit of thy temerity !   [*Pushes him forward.*

PETOU.

Ugh !   How I wish this guzzle were Dominique's.

RIGAUD.

Where is my sister ?

PETOU.

I came here to tell thee and thou hath stopped my wind. One good turn does not deserve a choking.

RIGAUD.

Speak out! I have worse in store for thee!

PETOU.

Then, as Monseigneur would say, peace to our rations. I have been authorized, instructed and prevailed upon by the aforesaid Monsgr. Dominique—by the way, the naughtiest wine imbiber in the army—to warn thee that the personal effects and good looks, with other incumbrances not now specified, are holden in hostage for thy good behavior.

RIGAUD.

Mon Dieu! Villain, when did this abduction take place?

PETOU.

Admirable—admirabilus, as Monseigneur would say. Oh, about ten hours ago and by this time the young mam'selle is safely in her prepared nest.

RIGAUD.

Lefebre, heavy must be the vengeance of God on

the heads of these wretches! Oh, Clarisse, pauvre
enfant! God protect thee until thy rescue.

PETOU.

[*Aside.*] How these mulattoes love their kin.
They must have hearts, after all—who knows. I will
have this to inform Dominique. [*Aloud.*] Oh,
though Dominique is carnal in all else and a glut-
tonous wine imbiber, he is perfectly virtuous. As for
myself, I think of naught else but prayers and inforced
fasting.

RIGAUD.

Enough, impertinent black! Tell thy master,
thy fellow clown, that Rigaud shall hold him in person responsible for this outrage. Tell him, also, that
if my sister suffer one insult to her virtue, all the
black blood in Haiti will not suffice to wash out the
wrong done her! State, moreover, that Rigaud is
answerable only to his God for his position in this
fight, and that his sword shall not be sheathed until
the government of France prevails throughout the
length and breadth of this island. Go!

PETOU.

Sacre bleu! They have got hearts. "State,
moreover," etc.

Mimicking RIGAUD, PETOU *struts off. Enter*
SOLDIER.

RIGAUD.

Take this letter to General Leclerc with our greetings. [*Exit* SOLDIER.] Now, dear friend, if our
judgment hath erred this day, may posterity deal
kindly with the memory of Rigaud. Adieu, until we
meet, where the deadly conflict's stern alarums bid
thought fly, and actions—deeds of valor, take their
place.

CURTAIN.

ACT II

ACT II

SCENE i.

[WILDWOODS. NIGHT. VOICE HEARD WITHOUT: "PETOU! PETOU! I SAY, THOU MISERABLE SCAMP, HOW SHALL I FIND THE ROAD IN THIS CIMMERIAN DARKNESS?"]

Enter DOMINIQUE.

DOMINIQUE.

I believe it is so written in my philosophy : "All roads lead to perdition." If this be so, what a consolation hath the unconvertible sinner. By my staff —and no such staff shall I weild when once I am the lord chancellor of this realm—this must be the main road; for between floundering in hogwallows and groping in prickly bushes, I find myself in a worse condition than is the soul of the heretic, Dessalines—if he hath one, which I have just cause to doubt. Ugh ! to make my condition worse that lean scamp Petou, whom I raised from an ordinary scullion to that of my respected socius; that hungry pauper, Petou, who never had the tender of a pour boire before, he became my attachè, and who should,

on such an occasion as this, be my staff, leaves me in
my dire extremities to be felled by the foul blasts of
this malarial swamp!   Ingratitude, O Petou!

Enter PETOU *blindly; butts* DOMINIQUE *squarely
in the stomach.* DOMINIQUE *falls.*

DOMINIQUE.

Oh! Thou uncanny pipestem! Thou foul blight
upon the name of man! Thou human sarcasm!
Come hither and help me to my feet!

PÉTOU.

Is there no forgiveness for me?

DOMINIQUE.

Help me to my feet, I say!

PETOU.

And myself to a beating at the same time, eh?

DOMINIQUE.

Oh! I will collar thee.

PETOU.

I've been collared once this day.

DOMINIQUE.

Ugh! I'm in a pool.

PETOU.

Scrubbing is, alone, necessary to make thee clean.

DOMINIQUE.

Thou fool! I'm wet!

PETOU.

The novelty of the situation must amuse thy high mightiness.

DOMINIQUE.

Ah! When as lord chancellor I have the ear of Dessalines, thy head shall go first.

PETOU.

I have risked it more than once for thee already. Thou wouldst be lord chancellor. Ha! ha!

DOMINIQUE.

And thou, infernal product of my generosity.

PETOU.

Is it possible?

DOMINIQUE.

Oh! how I'm fallen.

PETOU.

All in a lump.

DOMINIQUE.

Oh tempora! Hard times, these.

PETOU.

Indeed! Sayst thou forgiveness for me?

DOMINIQUE.

Never! I can preserve my dignity even as I am.

PETOU.

Know thyself.

DOMINIQUE.

Thou malapert! Thou infernal device of satan! I spit upon thee.

PETOU.

And on thy stomach, too.

DOMINIQUE.

Go! Leave me to my thoughts.

PETOU.

Ump ! Such thoughts !

DOMINIQUE.

They are not of thee, I promise.

PETOU.

Of thyself? Still worse.

DOMINIQUE.

Hence, caitiff, my misfortunes provoke thy vulgar mirth ! I'll find repose even in this slough of despond.

> *Sleeps.* PETOU *feels his capacious pouch with his foot.*

PETOU.

Oh, sanctimonious roué ! Would-be philosopher ! Human ponderosity ! Vice trembles in Haiti when thou hath thy fall. Like Deliah, will I clip thy strength and grow indulgent through thy misfortune. [PETOU *feels flask in* DOMINIQUE'S *breast potket.*] What is this ?

DOMINIQUE.

[*Sleepily.*] The philosopher's stone ; verily, Petou —the philosopher's stone.

PETOU.

He lies even in his sleep.   I'll help myself.
[*Stoops to secure flask*; DOMINIQUE *collars him.*

DOMINIQUE.

Oh, thou ill-odored wretch!   Thou garrulous ill
bred scamp! Thou infernal miscreant! By my hopes
of future reward, I have thee now.

PETOU *struggling to free himself lifts* DOMINIQUE
to his feet.

PETOU.

And what hurts me most, thou hath me agains
my will.

DOMINIQUE.

Such a beating thou shalt have, as thou wilt re
member to thy dying day.   [*Shakes* PETOU.

PETOU.

Oh, my stars!   Ordain my head should go, when
thou art chancellor of the realm; but spare me the
beating.

DOMINIQUE.

Infernal imp, thou deservest death!

SUPREME MOMENT OF DUEL BETWEEN DESSALINES AND RIGAUD.
Act IV, Scene 1. (Page 95.)

PETOU.

But thou art merciful; too generous by far—too generous to miss this grand chance to be magnanimous.

DOMINIQUE.

Ump!

PETOU.

Oft do I watch thee; thy bearing is so dignified; thy manner so lofty. Thou remindest me of——

DOMINIQUE.

Cease thy flattery; it will avail thee not.

PETOU.

Thy looks belie thy words. What kindly humor beams in thy mild blue eye. What prayerful earnestness in thy tout ensemble.

DOMINIQUE.

Cease tempter! [DOMINIQUE *lifts staff.*

PETOU.

Impossible! Who would dare tempt thee. Surely not mortal man.

DOMINIQUE.

Enough !

Pushes PETOU *from him. Lifts staff with both
hands, as if about to strike.*

PETOU.

Strike, my lord, with all thy strength ; strike as one
who would, with one fell blow, bury ambition with
hatred.

DOMINIQUE.

Speak, what meanst thou ?

PETOU.

If, by chance, thy blow were to kill—ah, bien !
Bid good-bye to thy—rather my eloquent memorial
to Dessalines, giving good reason why thou shouldst
be created lord chancellor of—of Port Au Prince.

DOMINIQUE.

[*Aside.*] Ump ! I did not think of that. [*Aloud.*]
Petou, mine is, as thou sayst, at times—at times
Petou, a tender and compassionate heart.   Wilt thou
do better, should I forgive thee ?

PETOU.

[*Aside.*]   Flies and roaches, too, are caught with

treacle. [*Aloud.*] Most assuredly, my lord. [*Aside.*] I'll not be caught again.

DOMINIQUE.

'Tis well thou art forgiven, rash man. But ever keep in mind, how near thou wert to—

PETOU.

Purgatory?

DOMINIQUE.

To hell.

PETOU.

Thou makest me shiver!

DOMINIQUE.

Petou, there be all else in that place that's evil save chills and shivers. Allons, mon ami, we have more serious affairs for the balance of this night.

PETOU.

Ah!

DOMINIQUE.

We have with us the maiden Clarisse, whose continued companionship has few charms for my sedate behavior. And truly it looks not well for me to travel long in close company with a beauteous member of the female sex. A mulattress, too, at that. Aye, in-deed, it is not well to have it known I have in my retinue—and that, too, unauthorized by Monsieur Dessalines, who loves not women ; neither good wine, God nor himself—a woman. Night and day, morn and evening, Dessalines cries "liberty!" It is his god—his fetich. Ha! ha! Petou, man dreams lib-erty is a life of freedom. Liberty—mark ye, Petou— for mortal man, is death. Conscience, then, availeth naught. So guard the portals of thy heart against the whim. Philosophy, Petou, philosophy—I'm in a quandary what to do with aforementioned female. Thou meddlesome fellow, I have thee to blame for this !

PETOU.

Her brother hath gold ; he will ransom her.

DOMINIQUE.

Gold, gold ! Thou sordid creature ! Knowst thou not, should the details of this abduction reach Des-salines, he would have thy ears for crows' meat? Why didst thou lie' to Rigaud and abduct this burden? Have I not already a herculean task to provide for thy necessities?

PETOU.

For that same reason, did I wish to provide for myself.

DOMINIQUE.

What wouldst thou with gold?

PETOU.

Get me the barrel of wine thou hath given me, in promise, for the last six months. I need a coat. This is no livery for the secrétaire. Secrétaire be —wet.

DOMINIQUE.

Coat! Thou needst brains more.

PETOU.

Even brains can be bought with fair promises. Hadst thou gold, how rich I would be!

DOMINIQUE.

Let me again tell thee, knave Petou, shouldst thou expect to become like unto myself, thou must in thy chrysalis state mortify the flesh. From women, strong drink—strong drink, thy weakness—richly spiced foods and fine feathers thou must abstain. Mark me well, the more thou refraineth now from the meats of Egypt the more wilt thou, eventually— when we have run the Franks from our midst—be able to thrive upon the marrow things of the world. World, sayth I? Nay, mundane sphere—'tis more philosophical. Wouldst thou some advice to thrive and be contented?

PETOU.

[*Aside.*] 'Tis all I ever get from him. [*Aloud.*] Thy pleasure, sir, to be—contented.

DOMINIQUE.

Well, says my philosophy : " Man is born of woman and liveth but a few days. He cometh up in the morning and is chopped down about nightfall. That joy which lasteth not long is a precious boon. To keep this boon the wise man maketh any sacrifice. Not so with the fool. He seeketh what he calls happiness ; he sometimes calls it liberty. In pursuit of the myth he loseth the substance." Ah, what gaineth thy stomach shouldst thou get the whole shoat and lose all thy teeth.

PETOU.

That is so.

DOMINIQUE.

Thy life is in constant danger [PETOU *gets closer to* DOMINIQUE] from corporeal dangers. The dangers of the corporeal life over which we have control are women, wine, rich foods and fine feathers. And the outgrowth of these dangers, dear Petou, constitute our spiritual ills. Strive to be contented, not

happy.   Long life means not fullness today and a
vacuum tomorrow.   Have faith in me ; be contented
with—hope, and be charitable to our present necessities.

PETOU.

Finis—for the present.

DOMINIQUE.

Hath thou heard all?

PETOU.

More than all—enough.

DOMINIQUE.

Then bring hither this maiden, and perhaps in the
interest of our cause, I will put to good use her
maidenly docility.

PETOU.

[*Aside.*]   Thy cause is rotten.   [*Exit* PETOU.

DOMINIQUE.

Some philosopher hath said it, and methinks his
application was wrong, that politics is the science of
government.   In my lexicon it is the science of downing—downing thy fellow man.   I believe my lexicon
is in common use.

Enter PETOU *and* CLARISSE.   PETOU *bows and struts off.*

CLARISSE.

Tell me, sir, why am I thy prisoner?

DOMINIQUE.

Not prisoner, sweet miss.   Prisoner—forsooth ! That would, in necessity, make me a jailor—a common jailor.

CLARISSE.

I do not understand this mockery.   I am decoyed from home, with the explanation my brother lies dangerously ill beyond these dismal swamps.   For five hours have I been wearied with this, seemingly endless, walk.   Thou claimst, I would judge by thy garb, to be a leader of thy kind.   Tell me then, sir, thy purpose with me !

DOMINIQUE.

Oh, woman !   Curb thy incomprehensible curiosity.

CLARISSE.

I am not, sir, idly curious to know thy purpose and my destination.

DOMINIQUE.

At most it is not meet time for thee to satisfy thy oft expressed desire.

CLARISSE.

Then, sir, it is not well for me to follow further.

DOMINIQUE.

'Tis woman's nature to be contrary. Yea, as my philosophy hath it—to be contrary.

CLARISSE.

It is not man's sphere to act the brute.

DOMINIQUE.

[*Aside.*] Not so mild after all. [*Aloud.*] I admire, sweet miss, thy philosophy as much as I admire thy piquant beauty. Beauty and wit, sometimes, go together—not always. Know ye then, it was decided at the council of the future rulers of this island—it was decided thou shouldst be the next prioress of the convent of Gonvaives and——

CLARISSE.

Sir, what sacrilege is this? What knew your council of me?

DOMINIQUE.

Ah maiden, thy fame for chastity and beauty is not confined to the narrow limits of one town.

CLARISSE.

Cease thy prattle, buffoon ! Thy noisome nothings ill befit thy garb of manhood. If thy purpose be to gain money by my abduction, send but a word to my brother and he will give thee gold.

DOMINIQUE.

Money ! Sayst thou money ? In times of bloody war and invasion, money, that is, currency, ceases to be a necessity, and its carriage becomes a burthen. See what thou wouldst have—and take it. Philosophy.

CLARISSE.

If it be not gold—what wouldst thou ?

DOMINIQUE.

Maiden, I have said : Thou hast been called and chosen. It is then for thee to be obedient in all things to the will of those who rule in matters of this kind.

CLARISSE.

Ah, I see, too well, I am the chosen victim of an outrage ! Holy Mother of God, protect thy handmaiden from the sacrilegious wretch who hath her in his keeping! Sir, I now comprehend my position; but I warn thee, I have a brother who will avenge my wrongs.

DOMINIQUE.

It is unseemly for one of thy gentle sex to utter threats of vengeance.

CLARISSE.

And how more unseemly is it, for thee to thus oppress me?

DOMINIQUE.

Maiden, thou wrongst me; verily, thou wrongst— [*Aside.*] Ah, here returns that lean scamp Petou! [*Aloud.*] I have said all there is to say. This night shalt thou, beneath the umbrageous foliage of yonder trees, find shelter; such a couch as is fit for a sylvan queen. Tonight, sweet dreams; tomorrow—ah, tomorrow. Adieu.

CLARISSE.

I will retire; but it is to pray thy machinations prove fruitless. [*Exit* CLARISSE. *Enter* PETOU.

DOMINIQUE.

Come hither, Petou! This suits me not; this incumbrance of weak femininity hath no charms for my habits of austere philosophy.   Petou, beware of woman, for her feebleness is her strength.   Man uses force; but she weaves more webs and digs more pit-falls than hath ever entered into the ingenuity of the imps of darkness.   Philosophy, my son—philosophy.

PETOU.

How different with wine——

DOMINIQUE.

Remember wine, women, richly spiced foods and fine feathers!   Thy weakness, Petou, Petou—thy weakness.

PETOU.

Eh!

DOMINIQUE.

Look me squarely in the eye and tell me truthfully, how shall we rid ourselves of this burthen?   Oh, woman?

PETOU.

Let her friends ransom her.

DOMINIQUE.

Fool!   Wouldst thou make matters worse?   This thing must not be known.   Should Dessalines learn of this affair, thy head would not suffice to pay the judgment.

PETOU.

How then?

DOMINIQUE.

Ah, how then! Petou, well said some erudite poet, "corn hath ears." Speak low, perchance these trees be so gifted. Canst thou, from out thy devilish ingenuity, devise some plan to rid us of this maiden, which leaves no ill odors behind?

PETOU.

I'll think—cogitate if it please thee. [*Aside.*] The murderous rascal. [*Aloud.*] I have a scheme if 'twill prove acceptable.

DOMINIQUE.

In emergencies like this there is no choice, my friend.

PETOU.

In the interior of this island there is a sect, who, clinging to the practice of their African sires, have in their religious rites a most heathenish practice.

DOMINIQUE.

When I'm lord chancellor I shall inquire more

minutely into this. I am moral, Petou, but not
religious; mark that. Go on!

PETOU.

Believing as they do in signs, spells and omens,
they from cabala conjure a temporal influence with
spiritual affairs.

DOMINIQUE.

Ah! I will note this.

PETOU.

On the waning of the moon they meet and in their
rites and observances they sacrifice human life.
Their place of meeting is within a stone throw of
this journey's end. Savez?

DOMINIQUE.

[*Aside.*] What a deep infernal rascal is this!
[*Aloud.*] I comprehend thy meaning quite readily.
Retire to the back of yonder tree! Sleep not; but
watch this maiden like the fierce bird would watch
its prey. With a clear conscience, pleasant thoughts.
Philosophy, Petou, philosophy. I will retire and
ponder on—my lord chancellorship.

> *Exit* DOMINIQUE *and* PETOU *in opposite directions.*
> PIERRE, *who has been in attentive espionage,*
> *dicloses himself.*

PIERRE.

What a pair of murderous scoundrels go there !
But their plots shall go awry ; for this very night shall
the potent Dessalines know all.   This is a war of right
contre might, and not a war on feeble woman !

SCENE 2.

WILD MOUNTAIN LANDSCAPE. TIME: NIGHT. THUNDER AND
LIGHTNING.   HUT, BEFORE WHICH IS FIRE, WITH SMOKING
CAULDRON.   OWL, CAT, SERPENT AND USUAL PARAPHER-
NALIA OF WITCHERY AROUND.

MERE MARGUERITE *feeding fire and occasionally, with
many cabalistic signs, dropping herbs and grasses
in cauldron.*   [*Slow Music.*]

MERE MARGUERITE.

'Tis the murmuring of the winds, evil winds ;
   'Tis the beating of the rain ;
'Tis the groaning of evil minds, evil minds—
   Pays tribute to my fane.
      In the herbs and grasses damp,
      From the field and from the swamp ;
      Where the serpent's deadly coil
      Breeds distemper in the soil ;

Dwells the antidote for death,
   And the preventitive of pain;
Dwell the silencer of breath,
   And the chiller of the brain.
In the silence of the night,
   Mid' the tombs and speechless dead,
Seek I emblems of my might;
   Find I symbols of my dead.
     'Tis a strange and mystic lore,
     In the depths of nature's store,
     Sacred to her chosen priest,
     Makes him king of man and beast.
     Oh ye mortals! Poor and proud,
     There's naught betwixt thee and shroud;
     When Marguerite exerts her skill
     By the *puissance* of her will.
     Serpent, obey the master mind!
     Get thee gone unto thy kind,
     Breed *disaffection* in the wind,
     Hatred and evils among mankind!

Now the hour approaches and those who in daylight shun Mère Marguerite and call her witch and conjuror, avoid her like one affected with a plague; now come to her humble as the dust. And wherefore? To beg her for some love philter. Ha! Ha! Or better still, some sure and sudden means of death. Oh, how many years have I lived in the shadows of yonder burning hill; and bred disorders among my former kind! By spells and conjurations have I set father against son, and mother against daughter.

The laughing babe has not escaped the evil eye of
vengeance. And I only sigh that, with one fell stroke,
I cannot set the world against itself! The cursed
humans! Little cause have I to love them; little
cause for pity or regret.—Ten short years ago I was
human too; but now all is changed. Vengeance
soured the milk of kindness; and I bear no kin to
aught save yonder companions of my hideous vigils!
Ten years ago, on such a night as this, left I the
haunts of man and found my way hither, to study in
the solitude of nature means for revenge. Revenge!
Ha! Ha! How sweet a remedy for all my ills!
Stoned like a dog from my former home; scoffed at,
jeered by my fellow slaves and ridiculed like some
damned offspring of Beelzebub, I was driven, as they
thought, out in the wilderness to die. And why?
Because my husband, child and master died within
one night from fevers, which they, fools, said were
caused by my spells. They lied most damnably!
—they lied! In all the simple weakness of a heart,
now dead forever, I loved my cooing babe and kind,
good man. I knew no hatred then; and now I know
no love.—Ten years ago on such a night as this,
scarred by rough usage, crippled, faint and half dead,
demented—'reft of sense and knowledge of the past,
I found here my haven, and here I stay until my fate
calls to the gods assigned me. Little do these friv-
olous fools, these superstitious followers of my occult
science, think that Mère Marguerite is she, who has
such just cause to curse their race! Murder, violence,

incest, every deed of hatred and inhumanity, every inspiration that bears upon its face the impress of hellish origin, find a faithful champion in me ! [*Noise without.*] Come on, ye fools !—Thrice cursed fools ; ye food for satan—ye beasts of prey !

> *Goes over to her cauldron and stirs. Enter* Blacks, [*soft music*] *fearfully tiptoeing.* Marguerite *appears not to notice them.*

FIRST BLACK.

Good Mère Marguerite, we, your followers, are here at your call to assist in the orgies of the night.

MERE MARGUERITE.

The what, knave ! Hast thou no other name for the sacred rites of thy sect?

SECOND BLACK.

Good mother, forgive Gaspard's slip of the tongue ; for well we know there is no more faithful believer in our cause than he.

MERE MARGUERITE.

Ugh ! Forgive is as strange a word to me as is all else that savors of human weakness. Are others without?

SECOND BLACK.

They are.

MERE MARGUERITE.

Then, as the moon is somewhat down, let's to the beginning of our festival.

Wild, weird music. Enter five men and five women, dressed in robes of beasts. MERE MARGUERITE *mounts pedestal with conjuror's staff in hand with which she occasionally stirs her cauldron, diffuses a red light. The ten men and women form a circle joining hands, and keep time to the music. Dancing around in a circle, first on one foot, then on the other. Chanting following wordless jargon in a weird moan.*

[CHANT.]

The preceding meaningless chant is kept up until from sheer fatigue the dancers fall on their faces and ten others take their places.

MERE MARGUERITE.

What would ye ask of him who reigns?

WORSHIPERS.

A goat! A goat!

MERE MARGUERITE.

Thrice asked, 'tis granted you.

WORSHIPERS.

A goat! A goat!

MERE MARGUERITE.

For sacrifice? What ask ye?

WORSHIPERS.

A goat! A goat!

MERE MARGUERITE.

'Twill be granted you.

WORSHIPERS.

A goat! A goat!

MERE MARGUERITE.

It yonder awaits you. [*Points to a cabin.*

WORSHIPERS.

A goat! A goat!

Two blacks enter hut and bring forth CLARISSE, *bound, gagged, pale and trembling.*

MERE MARGUERITE.

[*Aside.*] What? A maid this time! The scoundrel, Petou, promised me a babe and so stole he here and placed within my cabin this girl, unknown to me. [MERE MARGUERITE *comes close to* CLARISSE *and glares savagely and curiously in her face.* CLARISSE *shrinks from her.*] Ah! My beauteous dove, thou wouldst show thy strong aversion to my person. I had half a mind to spare thee. But 'tis as well. Thy kind are only fit to die or fill some lecherous master's bed. I hate thee for thy beauty; but 'twill soon be over with thee. Ha! Ha! [MERE MARGUERITE *assumes place on pedestal.*] What would ye now?

WORSHIPERS.

The goat! The goat!

MERE MARGUERITE.

Ye have the goat. Prepare the sacrifice!

Two worshipers prepare the stake to lash CLA-RISSE *to. Two start roughly to disrobe her of her outer garments. Tramp of numerous feet without. Enter* DESSALINES *attended by two* MAROONS *just as* CLARISSE *is about to be sacrificed.*

DESSALINES.

What mean these grewsome rites, thou limb of hell?

MERE MARGUERITE.

Choose well thy language, ere I hurl upon thy head a curse that will dry the very marrow of thy bones and make life a misery to thee. Away, unbeliever! Leave the chosen ones of Cabala to their rites. Or, if thou wouldst know what now we do—well, we sacrifice yonder mulattress to the gods.

DESSALINES.

[*Turning abruptly sees* CLARISSE *for the first time. With one bound he is by her side and with his sword bears off her captors.*] Spawn of hell, for this intended murder ye die! Dessalines has spoken.

Pierre, surround this den of serpents with our men,
and let no one escape. [*Exit* PIERRE. SOLDIERS *surround the men and women, release* CLARISSE, *who is
faint, and unconsciously leans on* DESSALINES' *shoulder
for support.* DESSALINES *turns to the worshipers, who
are thoroughly frightened in finding their interrupter
to be the much feared* DESSALINES.] Rapid is thought.
I decreed the death of all you; but it shall not be
so. Many here are but the ignorant dupes of yonder
unnatural woman. Then let the rest of you take her
and do by her as she would have done with this fair
and innocent girl. Pierre, remain here and see my
orders obeyed, whilst I hie me to camp.

PIERRE.

I will. [*Exit* PIERRE.

DESSALINES.

'Tis well that barbarous Dessalines with a hundred
thousand Franks at his heels hath not forgotten that
justice is the twin sister of freedom !

[*Exit* DESSALINES *and* CLARISSE.

SCENE 3.

[MOUNTAIN CAMP OF THE BLACKS. SOLDIERS SITTING IN
GROUPS. SPOILS OF THE RAID STREWN AROUND. ANDRE
AND PIERRE THROWING DICE FROM LARGE SILVER
DRINKING HORN. TIME, MORNING.]

PIERRE.

Parbleu ! What luck. I throw twenty-four, and

as sure as rain follows the clouds, you beat me one.
It is well I cease ere thou hath this good sword I
have sworn to sheathe in some Frankish heart.

ANDRÉ.

Better luck next time, comrade. You may win, who
knows ; all kinds of strange things happen now-a-days.
Only last night our chief returns to camp——

PIERRE.

Speak low !

ANDRÉ.

Ha ! Ha ! With a mulattress ; though I hate
them, I must own she is fair to look upon. But to
think that Dessalines, who hates a single drop of
French blood as the devil is said to hate holy water,
should at this late date assume protectorship of the
spawn. Ha ! Ha !

PIERRE.

It is your shake. Sacre bleu ! You beat me by
four. Ah ! I have another franc—I will risk it—
there. I throw the unlucky ivories. Twenty-six !
Beat that if you can.

ANDRÉ.

Twenty-four ! My luck changes. Allons, here
come the ones of whom we speak.

[*Enter* DESSALINES *and* CLARISSE.

DESSALINES.

Indeed, thine is a sorry tale of man's perfidy. Mark well my words, vengeance shall overtake these brutes, for such deeds shall not go unpunished.

CLARISSE.

Kind sir, how can I find words to thank thee for thy kind offices.

DESSALINES.

Maiden, I ask no thanks, for I have but done my duty. As soon as possible shalt thou return to thy friends at Port Au Prince, and shouldst thou feel some slight return is due me, tell them that Dessalines, the savage, barbarous Dessalines, wars alone on men and thinks it not beneath his duty to befriend their women.

CLARISSE.

Oh, sir, I pray thee think not too ill of those whose sires differ, but whose mothers are the same as thine.

DESSALINES.

They scorn their mothers.

CLARISSE.

Perchance they love not their sires more than thee.

DESSALINES.

If they love not their sires, why stand they in this fight shoulder to shoulder?

CLARISSE.

Were I deep in the lore of war, or knew I more than is the fortune of a poor orphan maid, perchance I could answer thee. But, of this I know, there is a just God who shall weigh us all in the balance, and they who are found wanting shall be cast aside.

DESSALINES.

Thou speaketh of the Christians. Should their gods prove potential—for 'tis in reason to believe the gods most favor those who build their altars and offer incense to their memories—then will the Franks and their mulatres win. But I, who am no believer in thy faith, fear no such results.

CLARISSE.

Were it possible thou couldst believe, how soon this cruel war would end!

DESSALINES.

At the price of liberty, perhaps; for doth not thy good book teach the slave obedience to the master's will?

CLARISSE.

Nay, sir. It teaches that obedience is expected

of the servant. The word slave, to my knowledge, doth not appear in manner such as that; for, if 'twere so, could the Israelites, who were His chosen people, thus rebel against their Egyptian masters?

DESSALINES.

Ump! This is new and strange to me. 'Tis different far then from what the masters taught. [*Aside.*] Methinks they lied.

CLARISSE.

And different taught with purpose. Oh! sir, could I but tell thee what I know of the good Christ and his trials, all for wicked man's salvation, thou wouldst soon perceive the difference between the truth and its perversion.

DESSALINES.

Of this wouldst thou teach me?

CLARISSE.

Aye, this and more; I would thee to pray.

DESSALINES.

Ha! Ha!

CLARISSE.

What, sir!

DESSALINES.

No offence to thee, kind maiden; but to teach

Dessalines to pray—ha! ha! ha! Forgive me; I mean no harm.

CLARISSE.

Sir, I see thou art in no serious mood. With thy permission, I will retire to my tent. [*Exit* CLARISSE.

DESSALINES.

Allons! The maid hath spirit, and it well becomes her, too. For me the lioness rather than the doe. I shall remind her of her promise, for I long to hear the tale of Christianity from a source so truthful—for surely those lips were never made to utter falsehood. Pierre, are the scoundrels taken?

PIERRE.

They are, my chief.

DESSALINES.

Bring them hither! I shall at once decide their fate. [*Exit* PIERRE. *Enter* SOLDIERS *who throw themselves on ground about dias. As* DESSALINES *is about to mount dias, enter* PIERRE *and* GUARD *with* DOMINIQUE *and* PETOU. *Both of the latter throw themselves at foot of dias and cry:* "Mercy!" "Mercy!"]
Mercy! Such mercy as hath the hawk for the fruits of his talons; such mercy as hath the ravenous wolf for the panting hare, or the cobra for the crushed victim of its coils! Mercy? Aye, such mercy as had ye for the Frankish maid. [*Seats himself.*] Speak

not of mercy, but tell me rather your choice of death,
To hang or burn.

DOMINIQUE.

Sir, I am not to blame !

PETOU.

Sir, we are not so much to blame.

DESSALINES.

Thou art a pair of blameless scoundrels. Carrion !

PETOU.

[*Striking his elbow in* DOMINIQUE's *stomach.*]   He
is speaking to you.

DOMINIQUE.

My lord, there kneels the inspiration of all my
wickedness. Ingratitude, oh, Petou !

PETOU.

My lord, there kneels the cause of all my misfortune !

DESSALINES.

Knaves and cowards, twin agency of evil. Sayst
thou, great hill of flesh, what right hast thou to
courtly raiment? For know I of no black lawyers
upon this island.

DOMINIQUE.

[*Aside.*] Courage, my heart! Here must I adjudicate all difference. [*Aloud.*] The same right thou hath to thy accoutrements of war, with this sole exception, I captured mine by stealth and thou thine by force. I served a judge, and this infernal scamp, Petou, was my scullion. When we received the glad tidings the slaves would yet be masters of this fair island, we rid ourselves of his lordship, and assisting myself to his vocation, became in faith as you see me.

DESSALINES.

I see thou art a hardened villain, given to naught else save guzzling, sleep and villainy! In times of war the country becomes one huge commissary to furnish all that is necessary for the achievement of victory; but thieves of character have no desire for the public good, and in consequence can give no excuse for their robbery. Thou, sirrah, hath no right to thy wig and frock! The cause of Haiti needs warriors!—Not such as thee. Disrobe! [*Soldiers unfrock* DOMINIQUE.]

DOMINIQUE.

Now, indeed, am I fallen!

PETOU.

Who'll be lord chancellor of Port Au Prince now?

DOMINIQUE.

Thou art worse than knave, pilferer of the dead! Again, good Dessalines, I beseech thee, mercy! Thou hath taken, dearer than all else, the instruments of mine ambition. My life can be of little value to thee; but the cause—thy cause—needs warriors. Accept me as a recruit to the ranks of freedom!

SOLDIERS.

Ha! ha!

PETOU.

Yes, kind Dessalines, send me to the rear; I am not ambitious.

DESSALINES.

Hither, Pierre. Go thou to the Frankish maid and give her the full import of these proceedings. I'll do as she wills. [*Exit* PIERRE.] Knaves, ye have no excuse to offer for your villainies—and none will I accept! My sentence is of death by the gun—a braver death than your misdeeds merit. [*To* DOMINIQUE.] Still, there is some promise your huge carcass will hold the contents of more than one. —Hither she comes. Make way, men! She holds within the hollow of her hand the fate of these wretches.

[*Enter* CLARISSE *and* PIERRE.

CLARISSE.

Sir, in obedience to thy commands came I hither.

DESSALINES.

Maiden, for thee I have no commands. Though ignorant of the honied terms and smooth deceit of those who rule, I am not forgetful that with women man's words should be clothed in gentleness. Before thee are two wretches, dyed deep in guilt, and thou, the sufferer by their iniquity. I have judged them, and decreed they must die. It is for thee, deeply wronged, to name their mode of death, to hang or to burn. For a warrior's death by the gun is no death for criminals.

CLARISSE.

If it please thee, neither.

DESSALINES.

Heard I aright?—Ah, then thou hath in thy mind some ignobler torture! Some slow and agonizing quietus that lets the victim linger 'twixt hope and despair!—Speak maiden, such death merit they! Thy decree is law.

CLARISSE.

I speak, great Dessalines, but it is for mercy.

DESSALINES.

Mercy, and these wretches! Nay, I must have misunderstood thee. Thy unfeeling persecutors;— thy would-be murderers. Speak again, maiden, what meanst thou?

CLARISSE.

Oh, sir, thou hath not misunderstood me! The mission of woman is one of gentleness and love. Man searches his cold, judicial mind for reasons; woman is guided by the promptings of her heart. These men, it is true, connived with evil design upon my life and person; but a merciful God who protects the helpless innocent, preserved me from their plots. As God was merciful to me, so would I be merciful to them and, pray thee, good Dessalines, to pardon them their intended wrongs upon me.

DOMINIQUE.

Kind maiden, thou hast my blessing!

PETOU.

Mine too; 'twill do thee as much good.

DESSALINES.

This is new and strange to me! Pardon—forgive. Maiden, is this the doctrine of thy faith?

CLARISSE.

And the teaching of my heart.

DESSALINES.

Unbind the villains! Turn them into the ranks; as soldiers I will use them—to stop hot shot!

RIGAUD. "——thy jewels—the crown of every maiden's life."—ACT 4, SCENE 1.

(Page 88.)

CLARISSE.

Oh clement Dessalines !

DESSALINES.

Is playing the fool.—But then forget—forgive.—It is to me a strange doctrine—I would learn more of it.   But, in all Haiti, of whom shall I learn?

CLARISSE.

If it so please thee—of me !

DESSALINES.

Of thee—perhaps, there be stranger things.   Of thee, then—shall I learn.

CURTAIN.

ACT III

ACT III

SCENE 1.

[CAMP OF THE MULATRES. TIME, 10:30 P. M. TENT OF RIGAUD, INSIDE VIEW. TABLE, UPON WHICH BURNS CANDLE. SENTINEL PACES IN REAR. RIGAUD SEATED AT TABLE PERUSING DOCUMENTS. REAR SCENE, MOUNTAINS AND CLIFFS.]

RIGAUD.

Thus is it twice, as I am about to give battle to the blacks and dislodge them from their stronghold, orders are sent me to await in camp, the further orders of the chef. This inactivity will lose to France her cause, and with it is lost all our confrères hoped to gain. These letters—there is much in them gives serious cause for thought: [*Reads*] "We have imported ten thousand of the fiercest Siberian bloodhounds, and these dogs will be a reserve corps to the army. Monsieur Lagarde, surgeon general, advises the canines' teeth be filed to a jagged edge, and then their work will be more effective. Employing dogs in warfare may not be exactly civilized mode"

—I should think not—" but we are dealing with rebellious slaves—black barbarians, and not civilized
men. France need have no compunction of conscience in adopting the most drastic remedies for the
blacks' disorder "—when did France ever have a
conscience—" Have it well understood by all of your
officers that the peremptory order of Count de
Rochambeau is that NO QUARTER be shown the rebellious blacks. Neither spare young nor old. France
desires no black prisoners." Mon Dieu ! Can this be
possible ! France, the home of chivalry and song ;
the home of culture and brave men, can engage in a
warfare so barbarous—so inhuman ! Never did I ·
regret more than I do now that I buckled on the
sword and swore allegiance to my father's government.

SENTINEL.

Who goes there?

[*Enter* LEFEBRE ; *grasps hand of* RIGAUD.

LEFEBRE.

Again, mon comrade, after a five month's separation
we meet. My lengthy communication reached you
some time ago, and from its length I judge you
thought I had plenty of spare time.

RIGAUD.

The obstacles to forwarding post direct caused your
kind letter to reach me only today. I have read it

over several times ; but the portion I have read most carefully, is the orders sent out by General Leclerc to the generals of arrondissements. The orders are worthy the brain and invention of the originator of the thumb screw and English maiden. It is barb-arous, Lefebre—it is infernal !

LEFEBRE.

Such is war. You have not then heard the latest news from Aux Cayes in reference to the French dog-soldiers, as the blacks very appropriately call the Siberian hounds?

RIGAUD.

I have not. The couriers I have sent out from this camp have never returned. Every mountain pass and every thicket between here and Port Au Prince contains a maroon sharpshooter. So all you tell me must be news.

LEFEBRE.

Allons ! As you already learn by my letter, the count general has imported a large number of blood hounds. These dogs are naturally fierce, but in order to make them more ferocious they are half starved. Twenty-five hundred of these dogs were sent to the commander at Aux Cayes. When Des-salines, who has a marauding army of blacks en-camped within a few miles of Aux Cayes, learned of the presence and purpose of these dog-soldiers, he

swore a heathenish oath that he would yet make the
French eat their dogs. On the night of August 25th,
a descent was made on the town by a large force of
blacks, led by Dessalines. The dogs were turned
loose and rushed furiously on the blacks. To the
astonishment of the garrison and its commander the
whole scene was suddenly illuminated; every black
had a pitch torch and rushed upon the dogs yelling
like so many demons, and so affrighted the hounds—
the dogs became panic stricken and rushed back
pell-mell to the garrison uttering fearful yelps. Since
that memorable night the dogs refuse to make a
charge. The blacks have gradually drawn a cordon
about the town. All roads to Aux Cayes are blocked ;
the supplies and provisions are cut off, and today
the inhabitants of that unhappy city are forced to
eat their dogs to ward off a miserable death by
starvation ! Thus has Dessalines kept his word—and
fresh dog meat at Aux Cayes is at a premium.

RIGAUD.

France will yet learn two can play at the same
game !

LEFEBRE.

I believe you. France has not a great advantage
in this fight, surrounded as she is by a thoroughly
united foe. To the honor of the blacks it at least
can be said they have yet to hang a black traitor.
How different with us ? Ah then ! Men in war, as

they are in the less sanguinary walks of life, are always anxious to protect self-interest. I am told this Dessalines is somewhat of a wit.

RIGAUD.

A savage beast who has not yet thrown off the wolfish covering given him by his mother in his native jungles! He wears an amulet of python teeth about his sable neck.

LEFEBRE.

True, Rigaud, but withal he is a humorous fellow. A bloody kind of barbaric humor, it is true. As an instance of this—a remarkable one—I've heard, is that since the successful charge on the garrison of Aux Cayes he hath adopted for his soldier's battle cry a very good imitation of a dog bark. When asked the meaning of such a peculiar rallying cry, he answered: "We have appealed to the Frenchman's heart and head; it has proven fruitless. We will now try his stomach." Morbleu! This Dessalines is a good one! But why so serious, mon ami?

RIGAUD.

So serious! There is little else in this war, to affect me otherwise. I think of our slaughtered brethren; our devastated plantations and the smoldering ruins of our once luxurious homes. What have the blacks to lose in this fight? If the event of battle go against them, they but return to their former state of servitude. Their treatment cannot prove more rigorous than it was formerly. Whereas, Lefebre, if France lose the fight, the mulattos of Haîti will be a people without a home—hated by the blacks and persecuted by the government he is striving so hard and honestly to uphold on this island. Indeed, I see no humorous side to these fighting times—an epoch in the history of the world which will figure in its darkest and bloodiest pages. And with all your debonair, ami chéri, I know that no one more than you comprehends these appalling truths that existing circumstances make so plain.

LEFEBRE.

Indeed, I do. I see the situation plainly; but I see it from a less gloomy view. If France win— ah bien—it will be the old time practice with her of breaking promises. If France lose—why French soil is good enough for me.

RIGAUD.

Yes, I fear it is with you as it is with many of our brethren, who prefer to saunter on the Boulevardes, loll in the foyers of the varieties and drive spirited horses on Bois de Boulogne, ogling fair women and exchanging bon mots with the shop girls, than to remain in Haîti contesting for the rights of men.

LEFEBRE.

Every man to his trade. Fighting a lot of savages,

at least, is not mine. Of one thing you can rest assured—I am with you to the end. In defeat or victory c'est toujour la même. But for the sake of health, if that alone, come into my sunshine.

RIGAUD.

My friend, you forget.

LEFEBRE.

Forget?

RIGAUD.

Aye, that Clarisse, my sister, is still the captive of that black brute, Dessalines. No sleep is there for me ; no dreams of pleasantry, such as you would picture in our enforced exile from our native land, until I have rescued Clarisse, who, next to my honor, is most dear to me.

LEFEBRE.

Ah, Rigaud, the very name of Clarisse awakens within me the most tender emotions. You love her with a brother's love ; think not that love for mother, sister or the laughing dimpled image of yourself can measure the height and breadth of my love for your sister. There is a flower which thrives as well in the humble fisherman's cot as in the artificial atmosphere of the gilded salons of Paris. Its perfume is redolent—all absorbing—overmastering. It makes earth a hell or earth a heaven, and makes man an

angel or changes him to a fiend ! The cowardly become brave ; the bravest oft become the most arrant
cowards.—I have basked in the sunshine of love,
and the only flower that thrives in this sterile heart
of mine is memory and—Clarisse. With thee I
pledge my life and honor she shall be free, and then
perchance—she'll be my own !

RIGAUD.

Enough ! Thy hand. Let us step without and
watch, as I often have, the descent of the moon behind the wood clad summit of yonder cliffs. [*Both
leave tent.* SENTINEL *wearily nods with back to tree
and permits them to pass unnoticed.*] Poor fellow,
he needs no discipline ; he needs a surcease from this
monotonous inactivity.

LEFEBRE.

Look, Rigaud ! Do you not see a moving form on
yonder summit, walking as if in a trance? See, he
nears the edge most dangerously ;—he pauses ;—note
his majestic form. Now he unwinds his cloak from
about him ;—he is a black. Soldier, thy gun—he is a
spy !

RIGAUD.

Nay wait, he sees us not ! He speaks and though
his features can not be plainly seen ; we will move
closer and hear his words.

DESSALINES.

[*Oblivious of his surroundings, speaks.*] It is cruel, Dessalines—'tis barbarous, Dessalines ; but no more cruel, no more barbarous than my examplers in this war! My cause is just and their cause is wrong. Mine are the deeds of the avenging gods that follow in the wake of crime. Their battles are to enslave and make of men beasts ; my battles are for human rights, and it is just my blows should fall the hardier. Then, 'tis meet in these fierce and bloody times men's nerves should be iron and their blood run colder than the trickling of yonder spring. Call me cruel ; call me barbarous ; but remember, Dessalines lives in times when warfare should be the trade of fiends, and I'll see to it the sharpened fangs of the Frankish bloodhounds are filed no keener than my wits to study cruel deeds of vengeance— and why not? I ask my heart, when these Franks harnessed in all contrivances of their boasted civilization, with bottomless mines of saltpetre wrung from the innermost bowels of the earth ; with weapons of steel tempered in the heat of the lightning's flash ; with engines of war that belch forth death— destroying hundreds with the bare lighting of a fuse ! —With all these arts, the result of centuries of study, the Franks have yet to learn the meaning of justice. Cruel, barbarous Dessalines—and why not ! They build temples to their gods by the stolen sweat of other's brows, and call them sacred ! Then 'tis but

in reason with them to enslave a weaker race and
prove, by sundry testaments of their gods, 'tis justice !
Ah ! to them, I will prove an apt and worthy pupil,
for out of the fertility of my brain shall spring a
thousand cruel tortures, and every torture shall be as
a hundred deaths.   No quarter ! cries the Frank ; no
quarter for the young ; no quarter for the grey haired
stooping sire ; no quarter for the devoted mother,
even to whose breast they clung in helpless infancy ;
nay, no quarter for the suckling babe ; for the maid-
ens of the race no quarter !—Brave men have sought
the schools of beasts and learned their lessons of
humanity in the dens of wolves !   From the graves
of the slaughtered dead a hundred thousand voices
cry revenge !   Methinks that in the stillness of the
night the foul owls of rapine cry revenge, while nature hides her face behind the rolling clouds and
echoes in her mountain passes and in the deep re-
cesses of the forests—revenge !   Ah ! Then to the
Franks, shall I—I, Dessalines—be their instrument
of fate.   In me—in me, Dessalines—shall they find
the embodiment of hatred—the never ceasing, sleepless enemy to their race, who shall turn their engines
of war back on themselves, and out of their every
deed of violence, shall spring a score of bloodier
incarnations !   Oh, France !   Pile up thy deeds of
ruthless violence !   Dig at the feet of every black a
grave so deep that the odor of his stenching carcass
can not spoil the pure breath of heaven.   Mow
down his ranks ; bind him as the reaper binds his

sheaves; make every stone a head stone that marks a grave; let every blade of grass mature in the rottenness of his black manes.—Aye! use stealth and perfidy; use torch and treachery, and bring your basest means to gain your bases tends, and then—pause ere the combat's over. Oh, France, go count thy victories! I—I, Dessalines, will count thy dead.

> DESSALINES *turns to retrace his footsteps*, SENTINEL *steps forward, takes deliberate aim and prepares to fire.*

RIGAUD.

At thy peril! Rigaud is a soldier—not an assassin!

CURTAIN.

ACT IV.

ACT IV

SCENE 1.

[PLAINS ABOUT TRIANON. SOUND OF MUSKETRY AND BATTLE. BUGLE CALL, CHEERS AND DRUM BEAT WITHOUT.]

[*Enter* RIGAUD, LEFEBRE *and* OFFICERS.]

RIGAUD.

Mark ye well, my friends, though this day may be lost to Fance, let us not speak of retreat while there is work to do. [*Signal guns heard in distance.*] Listen! The French have landed. Lefebre—to Neybra; three thousand as brave mulatres await thee there as ever bore arms! Montpensier, thou to La Croix! And thou, Egard, betake thyself to Archayo, as fast as horse can bear thee!

[*Enter* SOLDIER *hurriedly. Salutes* OFFICERS.

RIGAUD.

Whence come ye?

SOLDIER.

Neybra.

RIGAUD.

What news from Neybra?

SOLDIER.

Neybra has been evacuated by our troops.

RIGAUD.

Enough ! Stand aside ! Poltroons.
[*Enter* SOLDIER, *breathlessly. Salutes* OFFICERS.

RIGAUD.

And ye?

SOLDIER.

Archayo ! Archayo has fallen.

RIGAUD.

Traitors ! Who could win with such a force ! Ah
then—here comes another. [*Enter* SOLDIER *in
great disorder.*] More news of defeat?

SOLDIERS.

Aye, general ! La Croix has fallen and the blacks
have reinforcement.

RIGAUD.

Enough, my friends ! This day is, indeed, lost to
France. But, Clarisse, thou shalt be avenged upon
that black brute, Dessalines !

LEFEBRE.

Rigaud !

RIGAUD.

Lefebre !

LEFEBRE.

I will to La Croix—at once. Perchance, I may never return. If I return not—tell Clarisse, my last words—were of her.

RIGAUD.

Yes,—my sister ! Fare thee well, ami chéri, the last chapter in my life begins ! [LEFEBRE *and soldiers depart.*] This is indeed a fraticidal war, where justice refuses to smile upon the right ! For years the sore oppressed mulatres of this island have hung upon the honied words of France like hungry bees upon the tender petals of the rose, in the end to be robbed of the fruits of patience, love and labor. Ah—now I believe, had we not arrayed our cause aside France, and thus given countenance to her rape of truth and justice, victory would, this day, have rested on our banners ! As it is, the air is pregnant with omens of disaster, and before the sun sets on the golden tops of yonder hills, French rule will have ceased in Haïti ! Thus lose we our cause, for right-eousness buckled to the armor of unjust might, re-coils with it, and feels the full shock of God's dis-pleasure.

*Singing of Marseillaise without; tramp of passing
soldiers and huzzas.* Rigaud *stands in back-
ground.* Enter Dessalines.

DESSALINES.

Heroic deeds were done this day and history shall
enscroll upon her pages: Haiti free and the black
man's domination! The crimson tear of warh as
washed away the curse of years and all smiling nature
feels the thrill of a long drawn sigh of liberty! Ye
gods of my native land;—ye sylvan gods, who in
every jungle dwell,—most potential beings, laving
within the boiling waters of the equatorial streams,
and taking your grandeur from surrounding nature—
your fiat hath gone forth, your people will be free!
And to thee my sword—good sword—true and tried
steel, forged, perchance, by some Frankish dog, thy
purpose have I set at variance and turned thy sharpened edge from the black man's heart to that of our
oppressors,—I give the kiss of peace and place thee
in thy rest, the scabbard. Right nobly hath thou done
thy duty; right truly hath thou met thy aim!
Through corselet of steel; through breach defended
by strong cloth, hath thou probed and found the
Frankish heart! Wielded by this arm, strong in its
purpose, unfailing in its design to further the cause
of liberty—were it possible for thee to fail? Fail!
no; had my spring of life run dry; my head grown
dizzy with the mad combat; aye, had hell itself prevailed against me; had the grim spectre hied me to

the trammels of eternal darkness———thy cause ;
the cause of liberty would have found another champion ! Liberty ! Eternal inspiration of heroic deeds !
A principle nature implants in all her creatures !
Liberty, the birthright of all mankind. For a time
man may suppress thee, but thou art of eternal youth,
eternal being ; and when once aroused from thy
dreamy slumbers, oppression meets his sternest foe !
Thy armor is more strong ; thy assault is greater than
prejudice and racial hatred enthroned in all their
power ! [*Shouts and song heard in distance.*] Hark !
'tis the death knell of oppression, that rings loud and
clear upon the Frankish ear. At last ! at last ; fairest
germ of all the Antilles, thou art free !—The black
man's sovereignty, and Dessalines—ha ! ha !—the
sovereign. [RIGAUD *angrily steps forward.*

RIGAUD.

Dessalines, thou art?

DESSALINES.

I am he.

RIGAUD.

Then, infernal black, prepare to die ; for this day,
have I sworn, shall be thy last !

• DESSALINES.

Thine oath was false, boaster ! I know thee by no

name ; but by thy face, I know thou art a foe to liberty !—Draw !

RIGAUD.

My name and cause in this combat ! Thou shalt know. Ravisher, thou hath in thy possession, one who is my only kin—my sister. My name—hated by every black in Haiti—is Rigaud.

DESSALINES.

What—Rigaud !

RIGAUD.

Aye, the brother of thy victim, thou hast so deeply wronged !

DESSALINES.

[*Sheaths his sword.*] Slay me, if thou wilt, my sword shall never meet thine in deadly combat.

RIGAUD.

I am no murderer, slave ! I will take thy life, but only as would a man of honor, deeply wronged, wreak just vengeance on a foe.

DESSALINES.

My heart is bared to thee. If thou believeth thy cause just, strike ! I offer no armor to thy blows, save truth. For with my last breath I shall deny thy charge of intended wrong to thy sister.

RIGAUD.

Thou liest like satan ! Didst thou not by false representation and lying messages entice, from her home, my sister? Didst thou not, taking advantage of these times of bloody war, hold her, ostensibly, as a hostage for what thou, forsooth, called my behavior ! What other wrongs thou hath, by force and devilish machination, perpetrated on this maiden, I know not of, for I am not here for tardy explanation. I am here alone to seek revenge ; even that revenge must be poor compared with the enormity of thy misdeeds ! For, a thousand lives such as thine can not repay the world for the loss of one pure woman.

DESSALINES.

Verily, thou wrongst me.

RIGAUD.

Thy denials will not shield thee !

DESSALINES.

Of thy accusations, Rigaud, I am as innocent as thyself. Having done no wrong—I need no defense.

RIGAUD.

Thou liest ! To thy teeth, thou liest !

DESSALINES.

[*Aside.*] Courage, courage, Dessalines ! This

trial will prove thy greatest. [*Aloud.*] Rigaud, blinded by rage thou wrongst me.

RIGAUD.

Again, I say, draw and defend thyself! I will not parley with thee longer !

DESSALINES.

[*Aside.*] Maiden 'tis for thee, I endure all this— even unto death—for thee.

RIGAUD.

This last I warn thee ! Draw !

DESSALINES.

Why shouldst thou, thus, bay an unarmed man.

RIGAUD.

Ah ! I see thou wouldst not fight a foe thou believeth to be thy equal in prowess. Great Dessalines !—Great coward !

DESSALINES.

Enough ! Patience can bear no more ! Young man, thy blood be on thine own head !—En evant !

They advance and fight. RIGAUD'S *fierce on-slaughts are deftly parried. Music. Roar of artillery heard in distance.*

RIGAUD.

Demon, thou bearst no charmed life !

RIGAUD *makes thrust; is parried.* DESSALINES *wounds him and bears him down to ground.* CLARISSE *rushes in and throws herself on her knees at the side of* RIGAUD.

CLARISSE.

Brother !   Speak brother, tell, am I too late !   Oh ! Dessalines, is this the result of my labors and prayers ?

DESSALINES.

Nay, good lady—I know not how sorely wounded is thy kinsman, for I strove hard to avoid this combat. But that potent Being, of whom thou hath taught me much, willed it otherwise.   Farewell, ere consciousness returns, I will retire—to a scene my heart is in !

DESSALINES.

Gone !   Perhaps never to return !   Brother, do we meet at last, only to part again ?

RIGAUD *arises; supports himself heavily on* CLARISSE.

RIGAUD.

Nay, Clarisse, though deeply wronged, thou art still my sister, and at no time more than now needst thou a brother's protection.

CLARISSE.

But, Rigaud, thou art wounded !

RIGAUD.

Nay, sister, not so deeply in the flesh as in the heart.

CLARISSE.

Oh ! this fearful war.   How is it with thy cause ?

RIGAUD.

Lost, Clarisse, and with it every hope of our remaining in Haiti.   The blacks by force of number and the intrepidity of their leaders have won this fight—the fiercest and bloodiest recorded in history. But it is not of this I would speak.   Tell me, pauvre enfant, how deeply wert thou wronged by this infernal brute, Dessalines !   Tell me now, that I may live to visit such vengeance on his black deeds, as would in calmer moments,—make my soul blush to think upon !

CLARISSE.

Wronged, sayst thou ?   Nay, not wronged.

RIGAUD.

Heard I aright !   Or is it possible that grief—such grief as thine—has placed its searing blight upon thy virgin mind ?

CLARISSE.

Nay, brother, calmly and with the full import of thy words, I answer : he hath never wronged me. On the contrary, he hath, in no rude manner, been my kind protector, through all my vicissitudes, since last we were together.

RIGAUD.

'Tis strange and thy abductor, too !—Is it possible ?

CLARISSE.

Possible !

RIGAUD.

Aye, possible thou canst look upon thy brother's face without a blush !

CLARISSE.

Shame on thy cruelty ! Canst thou remember, wherein our lives together, thy sister e'er deceived thee ? Canst thou in thy judicious mind, find a single evidence of falsity in mine ? Ah ! hath it come to this—my first accuser is my brother ?

RIGAUD.

Clarisse ! Clarisse, canst thou forgive me ?

CLARISSE.

Ay ! and forget thy harsh words as if they never

were spoken.—But thy wounds, dear ! Let me bandage what may, indeed, prove to be a serious hurt.

RIGAUD.

Nay, I was but stunned and now I learn thou wert well protected in thy jewels—the crown of every maiden's life—I am twice well ! But let us rest on yonder moss covered log and there will I listen to the tale of thy captivity and miraculous escape from mortal hurt. [*Seat themselves on log, hand in hand.*] Now, sister, tell me all.

CLARISSE.

I will, and that briefly; for I have not much to tell. On the fourth of March, thou remembereth?

RIGAUD.

Can I ever forget?

CLARISSE.

Thou hadst been away from home all that day and the day before. Maman and I had listened to every footfall before our door in the hope 'twere thine. From early morn to the closing of the day we watched and waited, fearing to go upon the streets, as they were filled with rough soldiery. Oh ! brother, it was a sad, dreary watch we kept—two affrighted women, who trembled at the sounds of bloody conflict in the streets before our door, and feared each moment that quiet of our home would be invaded by the frantic slaves without. Dusk grew on us, we dared not light a lamp, but tremblingly awaited thy coming, in silence ; when suddenly we heard three loud raps upon the outer door and a low voice in respectful tones prayed admittance on business of importance. Against the advice of maman, I answered through the door and asked from whom he came. He answered, from thee.

RIGAUD.

And lied !

CLARISSE.

I admitted him at once, and he informed me that thou wert badly wounded in the woods beyond— sorely wounded—and begged my immediate attendance. Hurriedly, I bid maman au revoir, and followed his guidance. Wearily for hours I followed his silent lead—in the end to discover I was the victim of a well planned abduction. My abductors were two in number : a fat, sensual creature—a bouffon lawyer the principal, and my lying guide his worthy tool. The purpose of these men were at variance and the result was, I was given to that terrible creature, of whose horrible orgies the island is all ablaze. Margeret is, as thou knowst, of that sect who in all their festivals sacrifice human life. It was their purpose that I, in a similar manner, should be disposed.

RIGAUD.

Mon Dieu ! Pauvre enfant, how thou hath suffered !

CLARISSE.

And a merciful God hath been with me in all my trials !—I cannot well remember all the gruesome rites and savage ceremonial of that awful night, but well I remember, I was rescued from the sacrifice and my rescuer—was Dessalines. Fainting I was taken to the camp of my black befrienders, and at their hands, ever since, I have received, naught, save respect and kindliness.

RIGAUD.

And Dessalines?

CLARISSE.

To me, in all things, he was the chivalrous man ! And on the day after my rescue, he told me I was at liberty to leave the camp, whenever it were safe for me to leave. Thou hath since known the times have been unsafe to travel. Now, that I hear the war is over and piece reigns again in Haiti, we will, dear brother, remain together.

RIGAUD.

Peace reign in Haiti !—Never ! The blacks, the French and men of color can never live in peace, in

CLARISSE: "——*Behold thy handmaiden kneeling in suppliance before thy altar* '"—ACT IV, SCENE 2. (Page 111.)

Haiti !—Poor Lefebre, who was to have been thy be-
trothed, is, ere this, dead, and with him many brave
patriots, who sacrificed all for France. As for us,
dear one, we shall leave Haiti never to return !

CLARISSE.

Leave Haiti ?

RIGAUD.

Aye, leave this sin accursed island ; where all has
gone wrong with the cause of Frenchmen !

CLARISSE.

Nay, I can not leave as yet.

RIGAUD.

Can not leave as yet—what meanst thou ?

CLARISSE.

Brother, bear with me. I have made a vow in the
dead silence of the night at the altar of the Virgin
Mother, that I would dedicate my life to the conversion of my rescuer—I must keep my vow !

RIGAUD.

Convert Dessalines ?

CLARISSE.

Aye, reclaim a soul, whose majesty alone is blem-
ished, by the great shadow of its unbelief in our

Christian faith.   Thou hath seen his valor, and I—
I have seen that 'neath his visage, dark as night—
'neath the rough and blunt exterior of a soldier—
dwells a mind ripe for seeds of Christian good !   In
his fiercest moments, when fresh from the maddening
exchange of blows; begrimmed with the cannon's
smoke and bespattered with the crimson tear of life,
he hath been to me, always, a courteous gentleman.
And my woman's heart—unlike thy cold judicial
mind—tells me no man, who hath proper respect for
virtuous womanhood, can be evil to the core.   My
vow shall be kept, brother—my prayers shall be answered, and I shall yet live to see my labors rewarded !

RIGAUD.

Oh, Clarisse, can it be possible thou hath lost thy
heart to this black barbarian ! Tell me, girl ! [*Grasp-
ing her by the wrist.*]   Tell me !—ere the maddening
thought makes me forget we are of the same blood !—
Nay, thou art in more danger, than first I thought—
forswear thy oath !   And leave with me this night
this hellish place !

CLARISSE.

It can not be !   Thy work hath ended ; mine hath
but began.   I see the bright light of hope shaping
itself into a star of certainty.—I see, and with
prophetic sight, my fate is linked inseparably with
that of Dessalines !

RIGAUD.

Ah ! then, 'tis too true ;—thou loveth this man !

CLARISSE.

Aye, with all my heart; with all my soul—I love
him !

SCENE 2.

STREET IN PORT AU PRINCE. FRONT VIEW OF CATHEDRAL
NOTRE DAME. TIME—4 A. M. REQUIEM SUNG WITHIN
CHURCH.

Enter CLARISSE.

CLARISSE.

At last, here is what my aching heart most needs—
peace and utter forgetfulness of the past. Beside
the sacred altar will I kneel, and consecrate my life
to service for the holy church. How hard it is to
leave the world, so young ; so full of hope !—so rosy
with the hue of promise—so desolate for me ! For
I cannot forget the past, so easily. Still, there is
some pleasure in the thought, though at times, I was
fearful he meant me not well—though rude in manners and uncouth his speech, I knew the tender feelings of a manly man dwelt beneath the rough exterior.

First did I dread this man and sighed and prayed for my deliverance. But how soon the change! No fear or dread dwelt here; only a longing that I might be the means of softening all his woes—for surely sorrow, alone, could set the seal of ferocity upon his bravest acts. Though even in his fierceness is a charm, I wot not of, save it brings me nearer to my aim: to make him a convert to our holy church. Often times, have I wished him less rude of manners and less harsh in justice—never could I wish him more manly or more honorable.—For shame! Such thoughts within the shadow of the fate, that lies within. [*Places hand on door of church.*] Farewell, brother—farewell all earthly ties! It is not so hard to bid all else farewell, as it is to bid my unfortunate love—forever farewell!

> CLARISSE *enters church. Singing ceases. Loud huzzas without. " Vive la liberte." Enter* DOMINIQUE *with cook's apron, iron pot and soup ladle.*

DOMINIQUE.

Lord, how I'm fallen! Instead of a mine insignia of office, I view the shadows of my mind's past greatness, apparelled in an old greasy cook's apron. Parbleu! A common hewer of wood and a drawer of water. Third chapter, second verse of—fall of man. In other words, I'm floundering like some wounded leviathan, in my own tureen, in the weakest kind of mule broth. " Dominique."—Des

salines said, only yesterday. "Is at thy service sir,"—
answered I, in my most dulcet tones. "Thou deservest promotion! Thou art destined to go up higher."
At last, thought I, my merits are discovered even to
the eyes of this barbarian. Simply and with becom-
ing humility, I answered: "Yes, sir." "Yes," said
he, "shouldst thou continue to sell sugar out of the
commissary stores and rum at so much per gill, thou
wilt certainly go up higher." And then, he made a
fearful grimace—a ghastly expression of a man
strangling with a rope about his neck. Ugh! The
very thought makes me shudder!—Then Petou, that
uncanny pipe stem;—the most ungrateful wretch
never neglects an opportunity to address me: "Monseigneur, how's the bouillon?" "Monseigneur, thy
counsel—no, I mean a well done potato with the jacket
off, and mark ye, be quick about it." "Monseigneur,
what's the table d'hote today?"—Jackal! What a
sad commentary on the tendency of man's ambition
to always soar within the fell influence of a killing
frost! And often times, when his head is resting on
Olympus his pedal extremities are restings on the
edge of a mighty tureen; and lo!—between the
rising and setting of a single sun, he has sunk beneath
the surface of its greasy contents. Ugh! Such
thoughts!

[*Enter* PETOU.

PETOU.

Hello! Old fellow!

DOMINIQUE.

Old fellow !—Ye saints, how I am fallen !—Old fellow ! It has come to this. Old fellow ! Saith ye? Hello—creature !

PETOU.

Eh !

DOMINIQUE.

Eh me, no ehs ! Thou bastard offspring of my generosity ! I have no stomach for thy wit, and mark ye well, Petou, thy levity will yet land thee in hell.

PETOU.

Perchance, thou'll keep me company there.

DOMINIQUE.

Keep thee company? Aye, there be more of thy sort who form the paving stones of hell, for crushed greatness to wearily tread upon.

PETOU.

Dominique, I regret my hasty speech, for all hath gone wrong with thee. Thou hath tried thy ambition and found it worth not a sou.

DOMINIQUE.

Thou canst not decry it, for it enters not into the comprehension of thy brain, Petou, to master great things. Poor weak brain, Petou—poor weak brain.

PETOU.

[*Aside.*] He is always talking of himself.   Listen !
—I have a scheme.

DOMINIQUE.

A scheme ! Aye, a thin man for plotting, the
strong to defend ; so saith my book.   Out upon thy
schemes !   To this unhappy state were I brought by
thy schemes.

PETOU.

Riches lie within thy grasp.

DOMINIQUE.

Riches !

PETOU.

Hath not Dessalines promised the contents of this
church, to his soldiers.

DOMINIQUE.

Rob a church !   Nay, tempter.

PETOU.

Just think of it, golden candle-sticks and other
valuables, too numerous to mention.

DOMINIQUE.

Mention it not !

PETOU.

I'm told the chalices are golden and studded with rich gems—Wouldst thou the rude soldiers of Dessalines possessed these?

DOMINIQUE.

Oh, Lord !

PETOU.

I've seen a crosier of solid gold and several statues in the same metal.

DOMINIQUE.

Philosophy, where art thou !

PETOU.

Besides, the collection boxes.   One for the widows and afflicted women—

DOMINIQUE.

Peace, Petou !—peace.

PETOU.

—And five boxes for the orphans.

DOMINIQUE.

And I an orphan too.

PETOU.

How fortunate; both orphans; ever since our parents died.

DOMINIQUE.

What means wouldst thou devise to get the spoils, should I enter in thy—scheme?

PETOU.

We will rob the thieves and thereby escape the sacrilege of robbing the church.

DOMINIQUE.

Conscience—Oh ! conscience be still !

PETOU.

Now listen to my plan. By this time tomorrow this church will be thoroughly sacked. Great stores of the best things of the chase will be stored away in the tent of Dessalines ; drunk with wine and sur-- feited with the excitements of the day, everybody's slumbers will be sound ; then with a steady hand and swift foot we'll——

> *Enters* DESSALINES *deep in thought. Unnoticed* DOMINIQUE *and* PETOU *steal off stage.*

DESSALINES.

Out upon this folly ! What time hath Dessalines amid the sweet smell of battle ;—amid the clang of arms and bloody debate, for thoughts of woman! Still, think I must;—an all absorbing thought. Even in the combat's fierce embrace; when the mind should deal, alone, with stroke and counter stroke; charge and counter charge; advance and well directed retreat—with the tactics of war and not the whims and fancies of sickly sentiment, thoughts of this maiden quiets mad joy; dethrones reason from her high empire and makes me study mercy! What fetich hath this maid?—For I have heard of spells and charms these Franks doth use, to still the will and subserve their ends.—Last night, in the stillness of my tent, strove I hard to gain repose, when thoughts of her, forgetful of self, made me sigh to think—thought she as well of me. Sleep came not to my heavy eyes and dizzy brain; but like some ship upon a restless sea, tossed I in fearful uneasiness! Tired nature, at last, filled my mind with dreamy delirium and witching phantasy. It seemed she were mine, body and soul; we were inseparable—as one. She thought for me and I for her; I lived for her and she lived—for me! And when she sighed, I sighed, and it rent my soul with woe, to think my sorrows made her sad!—Yet seemed there joy in all of this; ecstatic bliss that raised my mind to greater things— made me forget Dessalines was fierce, not sad; and found only joy at the Frankish death!—It did appear, she whispered to me: "Farewell; we must part, forever."—Oh! What waves of sadness swept o'er my soul. I begged her—aye, Dessalines humbled to the dust—begged her tearfully not to go ; for life without her, were as day without a sun ! Oh ! hellish treachery to my country's needs—I knelt and wept.—Aye, from these eyes that in infancy never shed a tear and in manhood, hath made many foe blanch before the depth of hatred in their glare !—I bedewed her outstretched hands with the briny gush of my emotion. A dream !—'Tis true ; but in a dream, too much ! Whence this dream, from what source, within, upheaves this great volcano ? What treachery is this ? What spell, I ask my heart, hath made me captive to this maiden's wiles, must make me pause in thought, and thinking—free myself ! I would be free, and yet —I would be free. [*Exit* DESSALINES.

[INTERIOR OF CHURCH.]

CLARISSE *kneeling before the altar.* DESSALINES *leaning in thought behind pillar. At first sound of* CLARISSE'S *voice, he starts from pillar as if to interrupt her.*

CLARISSE.

Oh ! Mother of mercy, behold thy handmaiden kneeling in suppliance before thy altar ! From childhood—aye, with my first childish prattle, have I besought Thy kindly intercession,—to come to thee, when sorely tried and heavily burdened, have I been taught.

Thus come I to thee now.   This heart I give thee
is hardly mine to give.—Like those little insects with
gilded wings have fluttered in the alluring glare of
worldly light, and like them, have I fallen a victim to
my own   incautiousness.   An orphan   child, my
brother ere this in France; what solace is there,
save recourse to prayer, the balance of this life.—
Ah!   When first I met Dessalines, little thought I,
love—such love as mine—would supplant every other
affection.   I feared him and yet—I studied to assuage
all his woes, and lift, perchance, from mind and soul
its sinful gloom.   Little saw I the end—he still an
unbeliever and I his christian love!   Forgive, oh,
God!   the sacrilegious act,—I, who from childhood
always breathed Thy name with reverence, should
thus forget a duty, higher than that to man, and plight
my faith to one who loves not Thee.—Oh!   Dessalines!   couldst thou but believe, how different all
might have been !   Since it is not to be, the world,—
for me, loses all its attractiveness, and I shall end my
days in the holy peace of this cloister, where from
morn to night, my prayer shall be for thee.   Accept
then, Holy Spouse, thy handmaiden, who vows to
spend the remainder of her days——

[DESSALINES *steps forward.*

DESSALINES.

With me !

CLARISSE.

Dessalines !

DESSALINES.

Aye, sorely wounded dove, 'tis I.

CLARISSE.

Heardst thou all ?

DESSALINES.

Aye, what thou saidst and what my heart hath, already, told me.—Start not, maiden ! The chain that binds thee to me is riveted in my heart !—A heart, 'tis true, made of baser metal than thine own, gentle one ;—a heart wherein the seeds of kindness, love and and truth are but newly planted, canst not bear fruit compared with thine. But still—a heart that will ever prove true to thee as, it has proved to the cause of liberty.

CLARISSE.

Heardst thou my prayer, for thy conversion?

DESSALINES.

Thy prayer—aye ; and methinks, the great good God, to whom thou prayed, hath also heard !

CLARISSE.

Ave Maria ! Can it be possible, that at last—at last, thou believeth !

DESSALINES.

With all my heart, at last—I believe ! Here came

I, in the dead silence of early morn, ere the dewy
grass had met the rising sun, to meditate in the quiet
of this solemn place.—Review the story of my struggles,
reverses and ensanguined victories.—To meditate on
the emptiness of life and the vexed problems which
have rendered my eyes sleepless for many nights.
To seek, perhaps, in the deep philosophy of cause and
effect; to invade the tangled web of matter with the
keen rapier of a fearless hand. To bring certainty
from doubt and, mayhap, strengthen my barbarous
opposition to God's will. Thought I, here, in this
temple, raised to superstitions God by the greed of
man;—a huge subterfuge to enslave women's whims
and man's inborn weakness,—will I, Dessalines, without a qualm of conscience, sternly root out from
mind and soul the seed, so securely sown therein by
thee! Only yesterday I decided to turn this temple
over to the barbarous hands of my rude soldiery.
Impotent man! Aye, and I would stand and calmly
view the work, and gloat in diabolic pleasure at the
butchery of the priest, and the cries of the affrighted
nuns, and find music in the groans of the slaughtered
dead! Start not, maiden!—reason had left its
throne, in its stead, frenzy ran riot incrimsoned with
the lifeblood of nobler thought,—by stern rage, be-
reft of reason, forgot I, that even in the darkest hours
of our enslavement ranked with the stupid ox and
patient ass, here beside yon altar was one place where
the humble slave could kneel side by side with the
proud master. Here at least there were no slaves;

no masters, save the one Master of all mankind! Oh! Maiden, no longer do the accursed thoughts, of the past, find lodgment in my brain; today I have achieved my greatest victory :—Dessalines conquers himself!

CLARISSE.

[*Springing to his arms.*] Oh! Dessalines.

DESSALINES.

Clarisse, thou hath been more potent than the Franks.—Thou hath outgeneralled me.

Bugle call without. Cheers. Sound of muskets. Enter PIERRE.

DESSALINES.

What means that firing?

PIERRE.

If it please thee, chief; Dominique and Petou were caught entering the commissary stores, and I had them shot.

DESSALINES.

Such were my orders. 'Tis well.

PIERRE.

Chief, the troops are without, and impatient to enter here.

DESSALINES.

Thou needst not remind me of my promise. Go, tell them enter ! [*Exit* PIERRE.] Let me look into thy sweet face, dear one ; perchance the last time on earth.

CLARISSE.

Nay, speak not thus ; remember I have prayed for thee !

DESSALINES.

Prayed for me.—Ah, yes, then all is well. [*Bugle within. Enter troops with Haitien flag. Range themselves to left of* DESSALINES.] Friends and comrades of my many battles ! You have followed me in defeat and now in victory. I promised ye, this day, the spoils of battle well contested, within the portals of this church. I promised,—mark ye, Dessalines never breaks his word or falters in his duty—the riches of this sanctuary. They are yours ! Take them, but ere you engage in your work of riot and ruin,—slay Dessalines where now he stands !

SOLDIERS.

Never !

DESSALINES.

Your love doth conquor me. Then let us remember that freedom must always be inspired by——

CLARISSE.

Religion, love and mercy.

DESSALINES.

'Tis well then, that the religion which fostered in the slave the love of liberty and gave him the courage to contest the power of might—with the weapons of right, shall be hereafter—the proud heritage of every Haitien!

SOLDIERS.

Vive la liberté!

DESSALINES.

Fraternité et egalité!

SOLDIERS.

Vive!

SOLDIERS *march, singing Marseillaise. Return to center. Curtain rung down on last verse.*

FINIS

WENDELL PHILLIPS

TOUSSAINT L'OUVERTURE.

———

"From the moment he (Toussaint L' Ouverture) was betrayed, the negroes began to doubt the French, and rushed to arms. Soon every negro but Maurepas deserted the French. Leclerc summoned Maurepas to his side. He came, loyally bringing five hundred soldiers. Leclerc spiked his epaulettes to his shoulders, shot him, and flung him into the sea. He took his five hundred soldiers on shore, shot them on the edge of a pit, and tumbled them in. DESSALINES *from the mountain saw it, and, selecting five hundred French officers from his prisons, hung them on separate trees in sight of Leclerc's camp; and born, as I was, not far from Bunker Hill, I have yet found no reason to think he did wrong."*

HON. NORRIS WRIGHT CUNEY.

"My advice to the young men of the race is: 'Always take high grounds.'"

A TRIBUTE

TO

HAÏTIEN HEROISM

BY

HON. NORRIS WRIGHT CUNEY,

Member Republican National Executive Committee
for Texas.

A TRIBUTE TO HAITIEN HEROISM.

[CONTRIBUTED BY MR. CUNEY.]

Nations, not infrequently, have greatness thrust upon them, and leave a name in history which chance alone adorns. Is it possible that an independent state could exist, in its aboriginal barbarism, on the continent of Europe, fifty miles from Paris and on an equal distance in miles from the great centers of intelligence, thrift and trade—London and Berlin? Would not the advantages of environment influence the conditions of civilization outside the immediate centers? Is it impossible that England producing a Cromwell, that France should produce a Napoleon? That America, the haven of the oppressed of all the great nations of the Old World, should produce a Washington? Is it not possible that the great characters which go to make up the history of many truly great nations, from force of circumstances, could not have been otherwise than great, in face of great opportunities. Still the little island of Haiti, thousands of miles from the great centers of European civilization, with a population whose conditions and environments would supposedly force the great majority in a state of abject servility and pitiable degradation, produced men who, measured by the standard of inherent manliness, great achievements, a knowledge and practice of the right, were capable of producing in the person of Toussaint L'Overture the superior of a Washington, a Cromwell or a Napoleon. "For was not Washington a slave-holder, Cromwell unforgiving and Napoleon a man of blood and iron?" The equal of these great men in the tactics of war, he was their superior in the breadth and pro-

fundity of his humanity. Let us glance at the history of this
remarkable people, who in one day could throw aside the
shackles and gyves of an infamous slave state and the next day
pass the transition period of a great national name. First, it is
hardly necessary for me to say few historians have given the
world a true and unprejudiced record of the revolutionary warfare of the black slaves of Haiti, of their Herculean struggle
for freedom and the example of barbarity set by the French
masters in their endeavors to crush the rebellious slaves back
into a state of hopeless bondage. "Haiti, next to Cuba, is
the largest of the greater Antilles of the West Indies; it is
equi-distant from Porto Rico on the east and from Cuba and
Jamaica on the west, with the Caribbean sea on the south, and
open ocean on the north. Haiti lies in north latitude between
17° 37' and 20°, and in west longitude 68° 20' and 74° 37'
28·' The country, as its name implies, is mountainous. The
range is of volcanic origin. Cibao, believed to be the loftiest
summit, has an altitude of 7000 feet. The mountains are
heavily wooded, and said to be susceptible of cultivation almost
to their tops. With a soil well watered, and with a climate
tempered by the sea breezes, Haiti, as a whole, is, perhaps,
the most fertile spot in the West Indies. The productions are
coffee, logwood, mahogany, tobacco, cotton, cocoa, wax, gin-
ger and sugar, and mines of gold, silver, copper, tin and iron.
Within a little more than an age after the discovery of America,
the aborigines had been swept away by the remorseless cruelty
of the Spaniards." Its rare salubrity of climate, its luxuriant
vegetation, its poetic beauty and the general fertility pleased
the warm, lazy-blooded Castilian, and gave hopes of rest and
easy gain to the beauty-loving Frenchman. Here they found
nature had been most generous in her gifts; here they found a
bounteous harvest and little labor needed to gather it, so they
conceived the happy plan of turning the million free-born,
though savage natives, into slaves—thus introducing into America, ere the sombre clouds of Africa had descended on the
shores of Virginia, the damnable traffic in human flesh. We

are informed that so barbarous was the institution of slavery at this time, even difficult as it is to accredit, in less than twenty-five years the number, at first of one million natives, were reduced to the small number of sixty thousand. It was then that the importation of blacks suggested itself to the planters. The slave traffic was then commenced with the robbers and cut-throats of the Congo and the pirates of Guinea. For a number of years the importation of negroes amounted annually to twenty-five thousand, many of them being from the most war-like tribes of Africa. Before these were shipped they were branded with a redhot iron, bearing the name of the owner. Every barbarous device that cruel ingenuity could suggest was practiced on the enslaved people. In the meantime the Spanish colony of Dominica and the French colony of San Domingo grew in opulence and population, and at the commencement of the French revolution there were at least five hundred thousand slaves on the island, thirty thousand whites, and about the same number of mixed bloods or free colored people. Though the slave masters were inhuman in their dealings with the slave, their pride would not permit them to enslave one drop of their own blood; consequently every mixed blood or colored person was free born. In many instances, recognized by their white fathers, they were sent abroad and educated in the finest institutions of Europe. As this class grew in numbers, education and opulence, it became, in time, a serious menace to the institution of slavery, though many of these colored men were themselves slaveholders. They had visited France during that frenzied epoch of its history, when the cry was: "Down with the aristocracy, and up with the standard of man's equality." They had imbibed the philosophy of a Rousseau, La Martine and a Raynal; they had listened to Lafayette, and thirstily drank in the feverish words of Marat, Danton and Robespierre. They were armed with the weapons of a higher civilization; urged on by an irresistible impulse to be the potential equals of the masters, and prepared to combat the erroneous theory that God created the stations of master and slave.

I shall pass over the first embryonic struggles for equal rights and the heated discussions of the French assembly, when on one auspicious occasion Robespierre exclaimed: "Perish the colonies rather than a principle!" These were but embers in the great conflict which ultimately resulted in the overthrow of slavery on the island of Haiti. There existed, unhappily, little sympathy between the freemen of color and the blacks, and the former's effort, at first, were not in the direct line of manumission, but to establish for themselves civil and political rights which at the time they did not enjoy. Nevertheless, the efforts of the middle class bore a full fruition, and kindled a conflagration that took the blood of a hundred thousand lives to quench. Dr. Wells Brown, in his estimable work, "Rising Sun," says: "The slaves awoke as from an ominous dream and demanded their freedom with sword in hand. Gaining immediate success, and finding that their liberty would not be granted by the planters willingly, they rapidly increased in numbers, and in less than a week from its commencement the storm had swept over the whole plain of the north, from east to west and from the mountains to the sea. The splendid villas and rich plantations yielded to the furies of the devouring flames, so that the mountains, covered with smoke and burning cinders borne upward by the wind, looked like volcanoes, and the atmosphere as if on fire, resembled a furnace. Such was the outraged feelings of a people whose ancestry had been ruthlessly torn from their native land and sold in the shambles of San Domingo. While to terrify the blacks and convince them they could not be free, the planters were murdering them by the thousands." What a horrible warfare! The blacks, who by example had never been taught mercy, retaliated with fearful vengeance. While this description of barbarous warfare was on, the civilized world stood aghast at the atrocities of the war between master and slave. And no cruelty was sufficiently revolting; when the captured blacks were being broken over the wheel, tortured with fire, shot down and left there to rot under the festering sun of the tropics; when hatred was at its height, and the very

orb of day paled above the frightful scenes below, Toussaint
L'Overture made his appearance as the leader of his brethren.
At the beginning of the revolution of the slaves, Toussaint
was an humble slave who had learned to read and write, and
had always conducted himself in such a manner as to win the
confidence of all who knew him. Before he took part in the
warfare of his fellowslaves, he provided for the safety of his
master and family. As if by instinct, the blacks recognized
his eminent abilities and followed his leadership. From the
untrained and undisciplined slaves he made orderly soldiers.
He changed the ferocious battle cry of the blacks to a more
soul-inspiring and humane one. He brought order out of
chaos. From the hands of the masters he wrested arms for the
equipment of his troops, and in less than two months he had
nearly fifty thousand soldiers, in whose hearts fear had no lodgment and death no terrors. Under him fought Christophe and
Dessalines—less humane than he, but not less devoted to the
cause of freedom. Dessalines, the greater warrior of the two,
possessed the ferocity of the Nubian lion, the undaunted hero-
ism of the Spartan, and an unquenchable hatred of the whites.
Toussaint did away with summary vengeance and instituted
court martial trials. But the French were far more fiendish
in their excesses than were the blacks. Their prisoners of war
were given over to packs of bloodhounds and literally torn to
pieces; men who had not taken up arms were treated to the
rack; young men and boys were cast into boiling caldrons;
decrepit men and women were killed in cold blood, and innocent, laughing-eyed babes were torn from the breasts of their
frantic mothers and, by the French, thrown beneath the hoofs of
fiery horses. What pen can depict these horrors and do justice
to their diabolism.

Throughout these fierce struggles, Toussaint was always just
as Aristides, and as willing to lift down-trodden humanity to
the height of true manhood. "Of a kindly, Christian nature
he was like Joan of Arc; in the observances of camp discipline
and religious rites he was like Cromwell; brave and decisive of

action, he was like Washington; but never a Napoleon. After the peace of Amiens, when Bonaparte rested upon the laurels of his many victories, and thousands of his soldiers grew restless with inaction, he decided to give them occupation by fitting out an expedition to subjugate the rebellious blacks in Haiti. Fifty-four ships of war, with twenty-five thousand veteran soldiers, were sent to the island. "Veterans who had returned from Moscow with Napoleon; who had crossed the Alps and scaled its frozen heights; who had swum the frozen waters of the Volga, and fought beneath the shadows of the pyramids of Egypt;" veterans of an hundred battles, who had courted death on the Austrian plains, and who found music in the whistling minie balls and the thundering of heavy artillery. Such were the men who came to Haiti to fight the raw material of Toussaint's army.

How sublime are the words of the heroic Toussaint, when he witnesses the disembarkment on the Haitien shores, of this great host: "Here comes the enslavers of our race. All France is coming to San Domingo to try again to put fetters on our limbs." But not France, with all her troops, her veterans of the Rhine, the Alps and Tiber can extinguish the soul of the self-freed man. But why dwell longer on this conflict, which resulted in the institution of slavery being overthrown in San Domingo, and the establishment of the first government of the negro race in the civilization of the modern age. It is true that Toussaint died of inanition in a French dungeon, by the inhuman orders of the French emperor; but the government he established lives to this day, a monument of the possibilities of negro endeavor. Well has that great humanitarian and orator, Wendell Phillips, said, speaking of the Haitien: "In 1805 he said to the white men, 'This island is ours; not a white foot shall touch it.'" Side by side with him stood the South American republics, planted by the best blood of the countrymen of Lope de Vega and Cervantes. They topple over so often that you could no more daguerrotype their crumbling fragments than you could the waves of the ocean.   And yet, at their side, the negro has kept this island sacredly to himself.

I am indebted for most of the historical data herein to Wendell Phillips' lecture on Toussaint.   It is strange to me why some historian does not write a true history of this brave people.

FROM THE LETTER

OF

ABBÉ GRÉGOIRE,

Bishop of Loire and Cher, France,

TO THE

MEN OF COLOR IN THE WEST INDIES.

JUNE 8TH, 1791

"God Almighty comprehends all men in the circle of of His mercy. His love makes no distinction between them, but what arises from different degrees of their virtues. Can laws then, which ought to be an emana- tion of eternal justice, encourage so culpable a par- tiality? Can the government, whose duty it is to pro- tect alike all the members of the same great family, be the mother of one branch, and the stepmother only of the others?"

HON. FREDERICK DOUGLASS.

"The Sage of Anacostia."

ORATION

OF

Hon. Frederick Douglass,

EX-UNITED STATES MINISTER RESIDENT
TO THE REPUBLIC OF HAITI.

DELIVERED ON THE OCCASION OF THE DEDICA-
TION OF THE HAITIEN PAVILION AT
THE WORLD'S FAIR.

CHICAGO, ILL., JANUARY, 1893.

MR. DOUGLASS' SPEECH.

[PUBLISHED WITH PERMISSION OF MR. DOUGLASS FROM COPY OF ORIGINAL MANUSCRIPT.]

GENTLEMEN AND LADIES: The first part of my mission here today is to speak a few words of this pavilion. In taking possession of it, and dedicating it to the important purposes for which it has been erected within the grounds of the World's Columbian exposition, Mr. Charles A. Preston and myself, as the commissioners appointed by the government of Haiti to represent that government in all that belongs to such a mission in connection with the exposition, wish to express our satisfaction with the work thus far completed. There have been times, during the construction of this pavilion, when we were very apprehensive that its completion might be delayed to an inconvenient date. Solicitude on that point is now happily ended. The building which was once a thought, is now a fact, and speaks for itself. The vigor and punctuality of its builders are entitled to high praise. They made the building ready for our possession before we were in readiness to accept it.

That some pains has been taken to have this pavilion in keeping with the place it occupies, and to have it consistent with the character of the young nation it represents, is manifest. It is also equally manifest that it has been placed here at a considerable cost. It has required material aid to bring it into existence and to give to it the character and completeness which it possesses. It could not have been begun or finished without having behind it the motive power of money, as well as the influence of an enlightened mind and a liberal spirit. It is no disparagement to other patriotic citizens of Haiti who have taken an interest in the subject of the World's Columbian exposition, when I affirm that we have found these valuable and accessory qualities pre-eminently embodied in the president of the Republic of Haiti. His Excellency, General Hyppolite, has been the supreme motive power and the mainspring of the efforts by which this pavilion has found a place in these magnificent grounds. The moment that his attention was called to the importance of having his country well represented in this exposition, he comprehended the significance of the fact, and has faithfully and with all diligence endeavored to forward such measures as were necessary to attain this grand result. It is an evidence, not only of the high intelligence of President Hyppolite, but also of the confidence reposed in his judgment by his countrymen, that this building has taken its place amid the splendors and architectural wonders which have sprung up here, as if by magic, to dazzle and astonish the world. Whatsoever else may, by his detractors, be said of President Hyppolite, he has thoroughly vindicated his sagacity and his patriotism, by endeavoring to lead his country in the paths of peace, prosperity and glory. As for Haiti, herself, we may well say that, from the beginning of her national career until now, she has been true to herself, and has been wisely sensible of her surroundings. No act of her's is more creditable than that of her presence here. Never, when called by her right name, has she flinched. She has never been ashamed of her cause or of her color. Honored by an invitation from the government of the United States to take her place here, and to be represented among the foremost civilized nations of the earth, she did not quail or hesitate. Her presence here today is a proof that she has the courage and the ability to stand up and be counted in the great procession of our nineteenth century civilization.

Though this pavilion is modest in its dimensions and unpretending in its architectural style and proportions; though it may not bear favorable comparison with the buildings by which it is surrounded, and which are erected by more powerful nations, it will not, I dare say, be counted as in any sense unworthy of the high place which it occupies or of the people whose interests it represents.   The nations of the old world can count their years by thousands, their population by millions and their wealth by mountains of gold.   It was not to be expected that Haiti, with its restricted territory and its limited population and wealth, could here rival, or would try to rival the splendors created by those older nations, and yet I will be allowed to say for her, that it was in her power to have erected a building much larger and finer than the one we now occupy.   She has, however, wisely chosen to put no strain upon her resources, and has been perfectly satisfied to erect an edifice, admirably adapted to its uses and entirely respectable in its appearance. In this she has shown her good taste, not less than her good sense.

For ourselves as commissioners, under whose supervision and direction this pavilion has been erected, I may say that we feel sure that Haiti will heartily approve our work, and that no citizen of that country, who shall visit the World's Columbian exposition, will be ashamed of the appearance of this building, or will fail to look upon it and contemplate it with satisfied complacency.   Its internal appointments are consistent with its external appearance.   They bear the evidence of proper and thoughtful consideration for the taste, comfort and convenience of visitors, as well as for the appropriate display of the productions of the country, which shall be here exhibited.   Happy in these respects, it is equally happy in another.   Its location is a desirable one.   It is not a candle put under a bushel, but a city set upon a hill.   For this we cannot too much commend the liberality of the honorable commissioners and managers of these grounds.   They have awarded us ample space and a happy location.   They might have very easily consulted the customs and prejudices unhappily existing in certain parts of our country, and have relegated our little pavilion to an obscure and undesirable corner; but they have acted in the spirit of

human brotherhood, and in harmony with the grand idea un-
derlying this exposition. They have given us one of the very
best sites which could have been selected. Neither can we
complain of obscurity or of isolation. We are situated upon
one of the finest avenues of these grounds. Standing upon our
veranda, we may view one of the largest of our inland seas.
We may inhale its pure and refreshing breezes. We can contemplate its tranquil beauty in its calm, and its awful sublimity
and power, when its crested billows are swept by the storm.
The neighboring pavilions which surround us are the works and
exponent of the wealth and genius of the greatest nations on
earth. Here upon this grand highway, thus located, thus ele-
vated and thus surrounded, our unpretentious pavilion will be
sure to attract the attention of multitudes from all the civilized
countries on the globe, and no one of all of them, who shall
know the remarkable and thrilling events in the history of the
brave people here represented, will view it with other than
feelings of sympathy, respect and esteem.

Finally, Haiti will be happy to here meet and welcome her
friends. While the gates of the World's Columbian exposition shall be open, the doors of this pavilion shall be open,
and a warm welcome will be given to all who shall see fit to
honor us with their presence. Our welcome will be symbolized
by neither brandy nor wine. No intoxicants will be served
here, but we shall give all comers a generous taste of Haitien
coffee, made in the best manner by Haitien hands. This coffee
shall be found pleasant in flavor and delightful in aroma.
Here, as in the sunny clime of Haiti, we shall do honor to that
country's hospitality, a hospitality which permits no weary
traveler, setting foot upon her soil, to go away hungry or
thirsty. Whether upon her fertile plains or on the verdant
sides of her incomparable mountains; whether in the mansions
of the rich or in the cottages of the poor, the stranger is ever
made welcome to taste her wholesome bread, her fragrant fruits
and her delicious coffee. It is proposed that this same gener-

ous spirit shall pervade and characterize this pavilion during all the days that Haiti shall be represented on these ample grounds.

But, gentlemen, I am reminded that there is another important subject which should not, on this occasion, be passed over in silence. We meet, today, on the anniversary of the independence of Haiti, and it would be an unpardonable omission at this time, and in this place, not to remember with all honor this fact.

Considering what were the environments of Haiti ninety years ago; considering the antecedents of her people, both at home and in Africa; considering their ignorance, their weakness and their want of military training; considering their destitution of the munitions of war, and measuring the tremendous moral and material forces that confronted and opposed them, the achievement of their independence is one of the most remarkable and one of the most wonderful events in the history of this eventful century; and, I may almost say, in the history of mankind. The accomplishing of our American independence was a task of tremendous proportions. In the contemplation of it, the boldest held his breath, and many brave men shrank from it appalled. But as Herculean as was that task, and dreadful as were the hardships and sufferings it imposed, its terribleness was as nothing when compared with the appalling nature of the war which Haiti dared to wage for her freedom and her independence. Her success was a surprise and a standing astonishment to the world. Our war of the revolution had a thousand years of civilization behind it. The men who led it were descendents of statesmen and heroes. Their ancestry were the men who had defied the powers of royalty, and had wrested from an armed and reluctant king the grandest declaration of human rights ever given by man to the world. They possessed the knowledge and character naturally inherited from long years of personal and political freedom. They belonged to the ruling race of the world, and the sympathy of the world was with them. But far different was it with the men of Haiti. The world was all against them. They were slaves, accustomed to stand and tremble in the presence of haughty masters. Obedience to the will of others was their education, and their religion was patience and resignation to the rule of pride and cruelty. As a race, they stood before the world as the most abject, helpless and degraded of mankind. Yet, from these men of the negro race, came brave men; men who loved liberty more than life; wise men, statesmen, warriors and heroes; men whose deeds stamp them as worthy to rank with the greatest and noblest of mankind; men who gained their freedom and independence against odds as formidable as ever confronted a righteous cause or its advocates. Aye, and they not only gained their liberty and independence, but they have never surrendered what they gained to any power on earth. This precious inheritance they hold to-day, and I venture to assert here, in the ear of all the world, that they never will surrender that inheritance.

Much has been said of the savage and sanguinary character of the war waged by the Haitiens against their masters and against the invaders sent from France by Napoleon, with the purpose to re-enslave them. But impartial history records the fact, that every act of blood and torture committed by the Haitiens during that war, had been preluded by like atrocities on the part of the French. The revolutionists adopted the course essential to success in gaining their freedom and independence, and did what any other people assailed by such an enemy for such a purpose would likely have done. They met deception with deception; arms with arms; harassing warfare with harassing warfare; fire with fire; blood with blood; and they would never have gained their freedom and independence if they had not thus matched the French at all points.

History will be searched in vain for a warrior more humane; more free from the spirit of revenge; more disposed to protect his enemies, and less disposed to practice retaliation for acts of cruelty, than General Toussaint L'Overture. His motto, from the beginning of the war to the end of his participation in it,

was protection to the white colonists, and no retaliation of in-
juries No man in the island had been more loyal to France,
to the French Republic and to Napoleon Bonaparte; but when
he was compelled to believe that Napoleon was fitting out a
large fleet and was about to send a large army to Haiti to con-
quer his people and reduce them to slavery, he, like a true
patriot and a true man, determined to defeat this infernal purpose, by preparing for defense.

Standing on the heights of Cape Samana, he, with his
trusted generals, watched and waited for the arrival of the expected fleet conveying one of the best equipped and most formidable armies ever sent against a foe so comparatively weak and
helpless as Haiti then appeared to be. It was composed of
veteran troops; troops which had seen service on the Rhine;
troops which had carried French arms in glory to Egypt and
under the shadow of the eternal pyramids. Toussaint at last
beheld—one after another, to the number of fifty-four—the
ships of this powerful army come within the waters of his be-
loved country.

We will ever be able to measure the mental agony of this
man, as he stood on those heights and watched and waited for
this enemy coming with fetters and chains for the limbs of his
people and slave whips for their backs. What heart does not
ache in the contemplation of such misery?

It is not for me here to trace the course and particulars of the
then impending conflict, or to dwell upon the horrible features
which will mark it to all time as a conflict which can never be
contemplated but with a shudder. These must be left to history
and to the more impartial judgment of a wiser future.

ERRATA.

We beg leave to call the reader's attention to a few errors which have unavoidably crept into this edition, and for which we crave his kind indulgence. Aside from orthographic and rhetorical errors, the following are the most conspicuous: In Act IV. Scene 1, page 95, Dessalines' exit is left unmentioned, and he is made to speak once where it should have been Clarisse; also, on page 35, Act II, Scene 1, where "Delilah" is spelt "Deliah." We could mention others, but these, in our opinion, are the most unpardonable.

THE PUBLISHERS.